W I N N I N G
WORLD
WAR III

INDUSTRIAL STRENGTH COMPUTER SCIENCE

KENNETH JAMES HAMER-HODGES

STUDIO
OF BOOKS
THE SPACE FOR YOUR MESSAGE

Studio of Books LLC
5900 Balcones Drive Suite 100
Austin, Texas 78731
www.studioofbooks.org
Hotline: (254) 800-1183

Ordering Information:
Special discounts are available on quantity purchases by corporations, associations, and others. For details, contact the publisher at the address above.

Printed in the United States of America.

ISBN-13: Softcover   978-1-964864-98-3
          eBook   978-1-964864-99-0

Library of Congress Control Number: 2024926518

DEDICATION

To my Family, my Grandchildren, and to every future generation
that struggles with Cyberspace

INTRODUCTION

his book, the last of a trilogy on 'Industrial-Strength Computer Science,' concludes the exploration of scientifically engineered fail-safe computers. Computers engineered by the principles of the Church-Turing Thesis using the λ-calculus to control individual threads of computation as a machine. The λ-calculus is Professor Alonzo Church's masterpiece that he formulated while guiding his graduate student, Alan Turing, to invent the Turing machine. The two ideas work hand in glove together as a Church-Turing Machine as a flawless computer for the Information Age.

The binary computer that changed the world is from the Mechanical Age of World War II. Information and the λ-calculus were yet to be understood. The Mechanical Age won the war, so physics dictated the binary computer, not logic. Software and computer science did not understand or need the symbolic abstractions and logic of λ-calculus or digital privacy and information security.

Nevertheless, Turing's idea was framed and encapsulated by Alonzo's λ-calculus, a formula defining everything about computation as a science. Alonzo's λ-calculus is nature's science of atomic computation. It expresses the individuality of life from birth to death. It abstracts nature asfunctionality for computer science using the simple rules of λ-calculus. At the birth of civilization, the Abacus and in the 1600s, millenniums later, the logarithmic slide rule embedded the λ-calculus. Their simplicity democratizes computer science as a branch of mathematics and logic for anyone to understand. Successful computers flawlessly hide their implementation details inside the scientific symbolism of the λ-calculus.

Encapsulating the implementation hides these details from attack as an atomic structure. The science of λ-calculus, when applied to computers, detects malware on the spot, preventing the curse of malware, adds the considerable power of functional programming to the computer's machine code and removes the need for a central operating system. The cockpit of a binary computer is a jigsaw puzzle. In contrast, the cockpit of a Church-Turing computer is a fully instrumented flight control system with a pilot and a navigator crosschecking everything together.

Mistakes and attacks ignored by binary computers are caught. Malware is locked out, code errors are found immediately, criminals are prosecuted, ransomware is prevented, and cyber wars are won on the surface of computer science, inside the cockpit at the digital pinpoint where all the action occurs. The cockpit is the fulcrum of computer science, with a digital leaver long enough to move the world[1]. It is central to the future of humanity and the

progress of civilization, the crucible of the Information Age and the place where our digital future is forged. For life to progress, for individuals to thrive, for business to grow and for peace in the world, the cockpit of cyberspace must be engineered with the followers of Alan Turing as the pilot and Alonzo Church as the navigator. Only then will the Information Age begin.

This trilogy explains the transition from the Mechanical Age to the Information Age. Binary computers are the first flawed step that, without the λ-calculus, falls short of the science because, without the λ-calculus, binary computers fail the tests of time. Ultimately, the flaws of the binary computer lead to a dangerous, dictatorial, global cyberspace, an existential threat to society, the Bill of Rights, and every democracy worldwide. Not so for the Orwellian dictatorships

---

1   "Give me a lever long enough and a fulcrum on which to place it, and I shall move the world. "
— Archimedes

in Russia, China, Iran and North Korea. They thrive as authoritarian, surveillance states. The λ-calculus solves this dilemma. A novel, flawless design using capability-limited addressing in machine code secures the symbols of λ- calculus as golden tokens to digital objects. This reliably distributed software is essential to survive in cyberspace and sustain an untainted digital democracy for the endless progress of civilization.

This book evaluates the cost and steps for the successful transition from World War II's mechanical world to a Church-Turing Machine designed to win World War III and excel in the Information Age—winning the digital war that wages in Cyberspace. World war is always between good and evil, but the weapons are not mechanical. They are abstract digital implementations, programs, data, and malware that are exposed to the world by the binary computer. It is vital to digitally protect the data as individual abstractions of the endless information age, encapsulated by the λ-calculus where society is freed from hidden crimes and Orwellian dictators. The book identifies actions and costs required to preserve the U.S.A. as a constitutional democracy and prevent a catastrophic end to the grand American Experiment.

Table of Contents

THE IDEAS

This trilogy praises the advantages of Industrial-Strength Computer Science as essential for civilised life share cyberspace. The first book, 'Civilizing Cyberspace, The Fight for Digital Democracy' explains how this mess began and the technology pioneered in 1972 that solves the problem. Book 2, 'The Fate of AI Society, Civilizing Superhuman Cyberspace', reasons this change is vital to protect individuals, freedom, and democracy as progressive, cooperating nations. The rapid increase in threats posed by centralised binary computers and the rise of superhuman AI malware accentuate the moral and political consequences of failing to act. In this book, Book 3, "Winning World War III: The End Game in Cyberspace", the groundwork, method and costs for a national recovery plan are laid out.

The table below summarises essential terms and ideas the author uses to help those unfamiliar with the technicalities understand each term as intended and improve comprehension.

Term	Idea
Industrial Strength Computer Science	Computer hardware defined by the Church-Turing Thesis to enforce the laws of λ-calculus using fine-grained Capability-Limited-Object-Oriented-Machine-Code.

World War III	The global war conducted in cyberspace between good and evil human instincts is characterized as the endless fight between democracy and dictatorship, determining the future progress of civilization, nations, and humanity.
Malware	Malware is malicious software designed to harm, exploit, or otherwise compromise the functionality of a computer system. It can take multiple forms, including viruses, worms, trojans, spyware, and adware. Malware can infiltrate a system through various means, including email attachments, malicious websites, and software downloads. Once inside, it steals sensitive information, disrupts operations, or gains unauthorized access to the system.
Ransomware	Ransomware is a type of malware that attacks the single point of failure, the centralized operating system, encrypts the binary data and demands a ransom payment from the victim to restore access rights. It often spreads through phishing emails, malicious downloads, or exploiting vulnerabilities in software. Once the ransomware infects a system, it locks the user out of their data, displaying a ransom note with demands for a ransom, usually in cryptocurrency. Failure to pay the ransom is risky, slow, and expensive, and may permanently lose encrypted data. These attacks cannot be solved by patching software. They are a systemic feature of the one-sided binary computer and the superuser operating system that lacks a foolproof computational model.

The Church-Turing Thesis	A conjecture that human computation uses a finite set of rules performed either by the machine instructions of binary computers (originally the Turing machine) or the λ-calculus as a model of computation, using recursive functions. Founded on Alonzo Church's Lambda Calculus, it establishes immutable links between the mechanical and abstract worlds. Capability-Limited-Object-Oriented-Machine-Code binds software theory to a binary computer using Alonzo's scientific theory of λ-calculus.
Theoretical Mathematics	It is a pure science of abstract concepts that only exist in the mind, without physical attributes. The only criterion for judging mathematical objects is whether they are logically correct.
Computer Science	It translates the complex cognitive processes of Theoretical science into concrete, reproducible, and programmable phenomena with practical applications. The key is using symbols representing cognitive constructs of science and nature.
The (Lambda) λ-calculus	The λ-calculus is a mathematical system for manipulating abstract functions as named ideas implemented as digital objects. It is the scientific bridge between the abstract ideas of the mind and mathematics and the digital world of hardware and software. Alonzo Church invented the λ-calculus in the 1930s. At the same time, Alan Turing researched the Entscheidungsproblem (decision problem) posed by German mathematician David Hilbert in 1928 as a

	machine using instructions to express any computable function in science and nature, while the λ-calculus uses only variables, parentheses, abstraction, and application.
Entscheidungs-problem	The Entscheidungsproblem is a famous problem of mathematics and computer science posed by David Hilbert in 1928. The problem requires an algorithm to determine whether a first-order logic statement is universally valid. In other words, it asks for a way to decide whether a formula is true or provable within a given system.
Capability-based computers	A typed computer exemplified by the PP250 using Capability-Limited-Object-Oriented-Machine-Code as a logical symbolic address to enforce software security through functional modularity. Capability-based computers use unforgeable golden digital tokens that grant access to resources or services. It avoids the dangers of shared corruptible physical addressing used by binary computers.
Symbolic Computation	It is central to computer science and serves as the foundation of ideas like, but not limited to, theoretical mathematics, which is the ability to process symbols and perform functional calculations, as taught to children learning expressions for addition and subtraction. The computational model is formed by units of abstraction corresponding to the functions of the λ-calculus and the classes of object-oriented programming digitally protected by capability-limited hardware. A golden token and immutable digital reference

	define each abstraction. These Capability pointers are tokens or keys that grant or deny access rights to digital objects, following the principle of least privilege. Key owners can pass, inherit, delegate, or revoke capabilities.
Binary Computers	Binary computers use machine code statements using a shared physical address space. All attached devices are shared and guarded by physical conditions managed by the superuser operating system. Virtual Memory hardware and the superuser processes secure these digital objects mechanically. Symbolic elements only exist for programming languages, compilers, and the operating system superuser processes, creating overheads, complexity, and privileged hardware access rights that hackers and malware misuse. This additional software is unnecessary and has a dangerous overhead that exposes undetected and unresolved administration vulnerabilities. These single points of failure of centralized control can halt computers, networks, and software.
Turing Machine	An atomic machine that computes one programmed function at a time, as the engine of the individual λ-calculus functions in any expression.
Hacking	Binary computers using physical addresses cannot operate securely. Criminal activities and espionage infiltrate the foundational levels of computer science through undetected hacks that compromise the software safeguarding the centralised operating system.

Turing Commands	Binary RISC instructions like add and subtract, where variables are binary values selected by a physical address in the shared memory of a Binary computer
RISC	A Reduced Instruction Set Computer is a binary computer that uses simple instructions to execute quickly but adds memory and compiler support effort. In a binary computer, the memory address is a corruptible linear address space, allowing interference through shared memory and other hardware.
Church Instructions	The λ-calculus requires six logical instructions to initialize the namespace table as a private and secure namespace to ensure each computation thread operates in isolation by preventing unauthorized access and outside interference. Function Abstractions are bound dynamically to individual threads programmatically by golden tokens that can reach across the network, and Capability-Limited-Object-Oriented-Machine-Code, which includes the λ-calculus ability to treat functions as first- class citizens, passing them as arguments or returning them as values.
Namespace	A namespace is an abstraction for a set of unique names as symbols as a problem-oriented solution using Capability-Limited- Object-Oriented-Machine-Code. The namespace avoids conflicts and makes code readable and modular.

Thread	Computational threads are sequences of instructions that can be executed concurrently by a processor or a core. They allow for parallelism and multitasking in a program, which improves performance and responsiveness. Threads introduce challenges such as synchronisation, communication, and deadlock, which require careful design and implementation using Dykstra Flag abstractions.
Abstraction	Abstractions are a way of simplifying complex phenomena by focusing on essential features and ignoring the irrelevant details. Abstractions help design, understanding, and communication within systems and prevent opaque centralisation by incrementally distributing functionality, reducing complexity, and avoiding ambiguity. For example, an abstraction can be a hardware device driver, hiding the device from outsiders and avoiding dangerous centralized operating system privileges.
Function	A block of machine code as a reusable module to perform specific tasks. Functions take symbols as input parameters and return symbols as output values. They do not modify the program results as can happen due to unavoidable side effects on a binary computer that lead to malware.
Object	Digital objects are data structures with unique identifiers, types, and content. They can be stored, manipulated, and exchanged in distributed systems without losing their identity or integrity.

Code	A code block is a set of instructions a computer or other device can execute. Programming languages, like Objective-C, Python, Java, C++, or HTML, traditionally create code. Machine code is the most powerful of all programming languages.
Dijkstra Flag	Dijkstra Flags (Edsger W. Dijkstra in 1959) are privately shared digital abstractions used to synchronise and coordinate independent but related threads of computations using the functions Post and Wait. This abstraction replaces the time- sharing role of the central operating systems that created all the gaps, cracks, and voids in binary computers.
Post and Wait	These two scheduling functions are the synchronisation methods used by parallel computations as Threaded abstraction. One case posts a task to a shared queue and waits for a consumer thread to signal when the task is completed. Another posts a request for a worker thread and then waits for a reply containing the result or the request's status.
Church-Turing Machine	A secure, second-generation design for digital computers that adds six Church-Instruction to an atomic computer defined based on secure capability-limited addressing. The binary and capability data are foreign machine types that cannot be confused. This rule created a typed computer using Capability-Limited-Object-Oriented-Machine-Code.

Golden Tokens	Golden tokens define digital abstractions as immutable capability keys to unlock type-limited functional access rights to digital objects in a namespace of symbolic variables, functions, and resources required by λ-calculus abstraction. Abstractions are a unique set of objects. An autonomous, self-contained class of function abstractions can communicate and cooperate by passing first-class variables and results as digital keys, the Golden Tokens. The implements a Church-Turing Machine as the foundation of computer science to guarantee safety, security, and sustainability.
Need-to-know	The "need-to-know" is a security principle. It restricts information to those with an approved need and ensures that only necessary information is shared and kept under lock and key. The programmer controls the enhanced security, preventing unauthorised access.
IDE	An IDE is a software application that provides a complete set of tools and features for programmers to write, debug, test, and deploy their software. An IDE should include a source code editor, a compiler, an interpreter, a debugger, a profiler, a testing framework, a version control system, and a graphical user interface builder.

| Capability-Limited-Object-Oriented-Machine-Code | This approach to machine code creates cookie-cutter software as modular, secure, efficient, symbolic, and reliable components that interact and perform tasks without relying on a central authority or dangerous physical characteristics. This secure, reliable, and efficient alternative to binary machine code is because it hides shared physical limitations and the consequence of malware, bugs, errors, or unauthorized actions. It combines the power and simplicity of the λ-calculus with the security and modularity of capability-limited object-oriented programming as standardized λ-calculus computations to separate concerns symbolically. It creates clear divisions of responsibilities among calibrated software components. It does not rely on centralised, privileged authority, like an operating system, a superuser, a virtual machine or page-based virtual memory. Instead, it is a distributed and decentralised architecture that abstracts and hides complexity using golden tokens, the immutable capability key. |

SAFEGUARDING DEMOCRACY

I n an era where software and digital technology permeate every aspect of our lives, the definition of robust computer science must be strengthened and reinforced. The future depends on computer science, and Industrial-Strength Computer Science supports the complete needs of the Information Age for software to survive and flawlessly pass every test of time. The Information Age demands that symbolic addressing replace binary addressing to ensure programs are like mathematics and forever hidden from malware.

Consider the first program ever written, pioneered in 1843 by Ada Lovelace. She published her program as an appendix to her translation of "The Sketch of the Analytical Engine" by Luigi Federico Menabrea, who explained Charles Babbage's Analytical Engine. Ada's algorithm calculates numbers in the Bernoulli series, which are just twenty-five mathematical statements of equality. This program is pure mathematics translated into Babbage's machine code, as documented on a single sheet of paper.

Ada's symbolic statements still resonate today. Everything, both functions and variables, is defined by scientific symbols where the function endure forever. This example dramatically shows how robust and enduring software could be, resisting malware and lasting indefinitely.

However, digital dictators design binary computers to enforce digital obedience. This software is regularly upgraded to fix emerging malware attacks, but it can never solve the problem of ransomware and zero-day threats. Cybersociety remains vulnerable unless computer hardware evolves to address software errors dynamically. The centralized design of binary computers is from the mechanical age when the power of scientific symbols was never understood. Physical addressing is shared. It makes computers susceptible to mechanical vulnerabilities that undermine global cyberspace. Symbolic addressing is the cornerstone of the Information Age that increases the power, functionality and digital security of digital computers.

Binary computers display five significant problems:

1. The Single Point of Failure problem: Centralized operating systems in every mobile device and personal computer create a single point of failure, making these systems particularly vulnerable to cybercriminals, enemies, and unelected forces.

2. The Undetected Error problem: Binary computers are susceptible to many undetected digital errors that include data and code manipulation, hidden theft, fraud, forgery, and outside attacks. These vulnerabilities are exploited to disrupt essential or nonessential services.

3. The Ransomware problem: Ransomware exploits weaknesses in centralized operating systems, locking users out of their devices and demanding payments for access. This attack poses existential risks to life, businesses and national interests.

4. The Deep State problem: The reliance on these dictatorial systems allows unelected bureaucrats to misuse superuser privileges, leading to opaque complexity and unrecognized surveillance of society, undermining democracy.

5. The Dictatorship Problem: The existence of undetected errors harms society in two different ways, first through digital corruption and second through the erosion of democracy. As the fabric of society evolves, software automation leads

to digital dictatorship as Orwellian surveillance expands in and beyond cyberspace. Lack of trust leads to a national breakdown of democratic institutions, all replaced by dictatorial software in binary cyberspace.

It underscores the need for a paradigm shift to replace binary computers with Church-Turing Computers built on the λ-calculus. This approach automates the detection of every error using Capability-Limited-Object-Oriented-Machine-Code, protecting cyberspace from corruption, external interference, and human errors. It replaces centralized operating systems with symbolic, atomic controls of the λ-calculus, ensuring incremental, distributed power through immutable tokens as computer science's safe and secure machinery.

Safeguarding democracy and national security is essential to sustaining cybersociety. Scientifically engineered hardware and software abstractions atomically prevent the inherent puzzle of programming the binary computer using centralized operating systems. The shift is vital to safeguard democracy and transparently democratize computer science for all to use with impunity. Cyberspace then protects both the weak and the strong instead of enslaving citizens and societies and robbing them of their individuality.

The trilogy explains the essential aspects of the problems, emphasizing the vulnerabilities of traditional binary computers and the perils of undetected digital crimes. It advocates for scientifically engineered hardware and software that resists undetected corruption and outside attacks. Cyberspace 2.0 must protect society by detecting every software error that causes crimes, creates conflict, or allows attacks by accident and deliberate enemy actions.

By tracing the evolution of computing and highlighting the progress through critical scientific events, the trilogy underscores the traditions of success and failures of binary computers that created the urgent need for action to achieve Industrial-Strength Computer Science. Only Industrial-Strength Computer Science can immunize nations against the design flaws used by enemies, counterproductive forces of the deep state or an Orwellian surveillance state. As always, for the U.S.A., the goal is to have a government of the people, for the people, and by the people. It must, therefore, be so in cyberspace. It takes a paradigm shift in computer science to protect human rights through immutable digital tokens, ward off enemies and criminals and prevent stupid mistakes through fail-safe machine code.

There were no off-the-shelf computers when I graduated in 1967, so we started from nothing. Guided by Professor Sir Maurice Wilkes, we designed a symbolic instruction set for the Information Age. It used immutable golden tokens and applied the λ-calculus programming model enforced by the fail-safe instructions of Capability-Limited-Object-Oriented- Machine-Code. The PP250 was needed for secure, distributed computing, such as global telecommunications and battlefield communications. It cost the Plessey Company in the UK eight million pounds Stirling when fielded in 1972. It achieved the ideas of the Church- Turing Thesis and proved how to assemble and sustain reliable software without any single points of failure.

The trilogy's first volume, "Civilizing Cyberspace: The Fight for Digital Democracy," explains the design of the PP250, the prototype for Church-Turing Machines. The second book, "The Fate of AI Society: Civilizing Superhuman Cyberspace," addresses the extraordinary capabilities of AI and its dual-edged nature. The author warns of the super-human dangers posed by unregulated AI applications using binary computers, leading to opaque decision- making, unstoppable digital attacks and, worst of all, AI breakout.

The books advocate for a Capability-Limited-Object-Oriented-Machine-Code framework to ensure AI technologies are constrained responsibly and transparently, aligning with the principles of safeguarding democracy. The history explains how far we have yet to go and the importance of learning from mistakes to correct computer science as the flawless, fail- safe, distributed machinery of programmed function abstractions.

The books are for a broad audience, from seasoned professionals to every concerned citizen and legislators, presenting complex topics engagingly. This inclusive approach encourages readers to participate in discussions about the unresolved ethical implications of binary computers, the future of democracy, cybercrime, the breakout of AI, and the necessity of a solid foundation in computer science.

The motivation for Industrial Strength Computer Science addresses an intricate relationship between technology, science, society and civilization. By highlighting the vulnerabilities of traditional computing systems and the threats posed by ransomware and AI, the author underscores the urgent need for the scientific framework of robust computer science, as defined by the two inspired founding fathers in 1936. The call to action is clear: we must immunize civilization by returning to the Church-Turing Thesis as Industrial Strength Computer Science and protect against enemy digital advancements.

As resistance, corruption, and attacks proliferate, catastrophic consequences harm every individual user and the fabric of the national government. The books highlight how such vulnerabilities undermine democratic institutions, exploit and manipulate information, rewrite history, and create an autocratic surveillance society.

One of the most pressing issues to resolve is the impact of undetected ransomware, which usurps centralized operating systems of the binary computer, locking users out and demanding payments. This attack poses existential risks to businesses as well as national interests. The first book emphasizes that software must be trusted. {ndustrial strength programs check every line of code logically and physically. Put simply, blind trust is totally unacceptable for the long-term future of humanity.

The second book addresses AI's capabilities and dual-edged nature, warning of the dangers posed by unregulated AI development and how the modularity of the λ-calculus prevents AI breakout. This book's third volume outlines a comprehensive plan indicating the costs and steps to transition from binary computers to Industrial Strength Computer Science.

The science of the λ-calculus creates a flawlessly integrated development and execution environment (IDEE) built from Capability-Limited-Object-Oriented-Machine-Code. This arrangement is summarized in Table 1, which outlines how Industrial-Strength

Networked Computer Science includes a fail-safe integrated development and execution environment of immutable tokens and function-tight networked abstractions, avoiding the vulnerabilities of binary computers.

Figure 1 Industrial-Strength Networked Computer Science (on the right) includes a Fail-Safe Integrated Development and Execution Environment (FSIDEE)

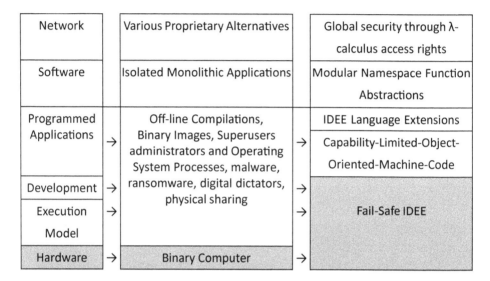

Network	Various Proprietary Alternatives	Global security through λ-calculus access rights
Software	Isolated Monolithic Applications	Modular Namespace Function Abstractions
Programmed Applications →	Off-line Compilations, Binary Images, Superusers administrators and Operating System Processes, malware, ransomware, digital dictators, physical sharing	IDEE Language Extensions
	→	→ Capability-Limited-Object-Oriented-Machine-Code
Development →		→
Execution →		→ Fail-Safe IDEE
Model		
Hardware →	Binary Computer →	

Exploring this transition from a traditional democratic society, which is governed by the laws of democracy, to a global cybersociety governed by transparent software to meet the national requirements independently requires the machine code to change from an opaque puzzle to the digital machinery of a built-in, to the Fail-Safe Integrated Development and Execution Environment (FSIDEE) of the λ-calculus. It is outlined in Figure 1 Industrial- Strength Networked Computer Science (on the right) includes a Fail-Safe Integrated Development and Execution Environment (FSIDEE).

In this way, Capability-Limited-Object-Oriented-Machine-Code enables the hardware to catch up and keep pace with software progress to prevent malware and AI breakout and remove digital dictatorship. The author advocates this path that leads to democracy over dictatorship by decentralizing and distributing software as the modular digital objects of individual function abstractions accessed by the golden tokens of symbolic addressing.

Binary computers, originating in the mechanical age post-World War II, ignored the λ- calculus science from 1936. With World War III now being fought in cyberspace, the solution lies in recognizing software as abstract ideas with boundaries to control AI-empowered nations free from dictatorial binary corruption. These golden tokens can represent the ideas of the human mind by name and location in a namespace. The namespace is home to a set of ideas, the primary namespace being mathematics. There are others for every branch of science, arts, and everything else in life around the world.

The author's first book in 2020, "Civilizing Cyberspace: The Fight for Digital Democracy," introduces the need for Industrial Strength Computer Science to safeguard digital society. It warns of the dire outcomes if hardware fails to adapt to AI software and advanced malware innovations, clarifying the dangers of general-purpose computers and their threat to society.

The scientific solution to corruption lies in the Church-Turing Thesis, which avoids centralized controls, ensures reliable software, and upholds democratic principles in cyberspace. The 21st century must leave behind the hardware perils of the mechanical age to end the threats of crime and Orwellian control.

In 2023, "The Fate of AI Society: Civilizing Superhuman Cyberspace" addresses problems from obsolete hardware, the risks of malware, and centralized management. It details the complications related to outmoded hardware and emphasizes the need for hardware advancements to match AI software innovations.

These books received five-star reviews, and the current book focuses on the cost and the need for action at the intersection of computer science and digital society. The question is whether we want an Orwellian dictatorship or a democratic cyber society founded on the US Constitution.

This book, "Winning World War III: The End Game in Cyberspace", lays the groundwork for a national salvation plan, concluding the "what, why, and how" of this trilogy to transition to

Industrial-Strength Computer Science. The goal is to fix systemic flaws in outdated binary computers and create a safe and secure cyberspace.

Appendix A is the author's 1976 presentation on privacy and security at ICCC, drawing analogies between natural solutions and the design of capability-based computers. Appendix B is his presentation at the 6th ACM Symposium on Operating System Principles, highlighting the idea of golden tokens for secure networked abstractions.

Despite the industry's attachment to centralized operating systems, the author argues for recognizing the power of Capability-Limited-Object-Oriented-Machine-Code for networked abstractions, programmer freedom and software equality as the foundation of a democratic Information Age society supporting flawless, fail-safe digital security and individual privacy. Industrial-Strength Computer Science is vital for cyberspace as a global platform. Congress must act; it cannot stand and watch enemy states win World War III, the Bill of Rights being shredded by the software from digital dictators, and the loss of constitutional democratic control all because binary cyberspace hides cybercrimes and favours centralized government dictatorship.

INDUSTRIAL STRENGTH COMPUTER SCIENCE

Industrial-Strength Computer Science is founded on the Church-Turing Thesis—the science of computer science. In convincing depth and detail that anyone can grasp, the hidden, sloppy dangers of binary computers leading to a disastrous end game are resolved. This end game is now playing out with disasters like the industrial freeze on July 19th, 2024, when the security firm CrowdStrike froze the world of Windows computers with a flawed update. A single point of failure that shocked the nation, repeating through binary cyberspace forever.

The nation must choose between depending on flawed binary computers that cause industrial catastrophes and only lead to dictatorship or making a strategic change to secure the eternal digital future. Industrial-strength computer science stands out as the only way to save the nation, particularly the USA, the leading democratic superpower, by adopting the flawless science of Church-Turing Machines.

Subject/Source	John von Neumann	Alonzo Church & Alan Turing
First Implementation	ENIAC 1945	PP250 1972
Memory Access	Virtual Memory Paging	Golden Tokens
Applications	Shift Driven Business Mainframes	Uninterrupted Global Telecommunications
Development & Test	Off-line Language Compiler & Test	FSIDEE + Language Extensions
Computational Model	Proprietary Centralized Brands of Dictatorship	λ-calculus Namespace
Addressing	Shared Physical Address	Capability-Limited Object-Oriented-Machine-Code
Hardware	Binary Machine Code	
Industrial-Strength Computer Science	Never	

Table 1. John von Neumann chose the Path of computer science in 1945 by ignoring the science from 1936

As shown in Table 1. John von Neumann chose the Path of computer science in 1945 by ignoring the science from 1936. This choice is a shortcut into a baren binary dead-ended canyon only fit for stand-alone mainframes. He wanted to be first, so he ignored the universal science of his Princeton colleague Alonzo Church from 1936. His cutoff is like the one taken by the Donner Party that does not go the distance in time. It digitally freezes unwitting networking pioneers to death.

Binary words, bytes, and bits are all the von Neumann architecture that is regularly misunderstood. Later, a central operating system was ordained as a superuser and a dictator to limit misunderstanding and duplications, save effort, and run backward compatibility to limit code regeneration. This digital dictator evolved into an unelected system Administrator who, as a single point of failure in networked cyberspace, can stop the world.

Binary computers are all branded designs—proprietary creations for time-sharing, memory management, input, and output control. Offline compilers and a dictatorial operating system do everything else. It leaves the binary computer flawed in critical structural ways. Nothing can be scientifically guaranteed when malware lurks around every corner. The proprietary foundation is unsafe. It is an unscientific contraption balanced on a single point of failure. It is an opaque digital puzzle for every individual programmer, not a scientifically engineered machine for nonstop digital computations—a machine designed to span the world and scientifically withstand every worst-case condition. As a new fact of life, the core of the Information Age, cyberspace must be as stable as New York's skyscrapers and scientifically engineered as the F-16V[2]. A global platform where advanced hardware mates with advanced software to survive reliably for generations and win World War III against worst-case superhuman malware attacks is all repelled on the spot by a trusted, transparent, engineered design.

When binary computers began at the end of the mechanical age after World War II, they were physically locked in rooms and guarded by expert teams who kept them running each day. This first-generation design has logical gaps, digital cracks, and scientific voids, allowing malware to exist and remain undetected. All these flaws remain toxically mixed with undetected malware, unpunished criminals, and dangerous enemies. They are the unavoidable consequence of a physically shared binary computer architecture. In particular, the hardware privileges of the superuser as a central operating system create a single failure point. One mistake can bring the house down, as happened on the 19th of July 2024, causing a week of airline and

---

2   F-16V: The Most Technologically Advanced 4th Generation Fighter in the World

other problems. Enemies, spies, criminals, and anyone else attack this inherent weakness to gain the upper hand, take control, scramble the data, demand a ransom, or attack the digital infrastructure of the nation and critical national services.

It is only a matter of time before a silly mistake or a careful plan stops the show. To implement such evil plans, enemies hide malware deep in the Homeland to facilitate their success. Nations are all secretly working in advance on these attacks to rout their enemies, beat their competitors, and subdue citizens through cyberspace when the time comes. These threats demand that cyberspace be fail-safe and that democracy functions as intended, individually and independently. Undetected errors and best-effort alternatives, particularly any single point of failure, are unacceptable. The USA and other digital societies that are all different in detail cannot build upon a one-size-fits-all centralized dictatorship.

Life now depends on global cyberspace's flawless, fail-safe functioning for everyone, skilled and unskilled.

The systemic flaws are caused by centralisation, unchecked errors, and shared hardware beyond control. Neither the user nor the programmer can stop these attacks. This centralised architecture that started after World War II was amended for the mainframe age with additional hardware for virtual memory protected by a centralised superuser operating system. None of this autocratic setup of unfair digital power that only leads to dictatorship is required by the science of computer science, defined in 1936 by the λ-calculus. The λ- calculus is the foundation of mathematics researched by Alonzo Church, Alan Turing's tutor, as Alan earned his doctorate and proposed his binary computer while studying at Princeton University. Their results fit together hand-in-glove, solving the flaws of cyberspace. The hand is Turing's binary computer, while the glove is Alonzo's λ-calculus. The encapsulated combination creates a flawless, fail-safe, scientific Church-Turing Machine that hides the binary implementation within the λ-calculus architecture.

The same dangerously shared mainframe hardware continues today packaged as the latest AMD or Intel semiconductor, still lacking digital security and the networked readiness of the λ-calculus. All too easily, administrators and worse network security providers like CrowdStrike make tragic operational mistakes, or crooks, spies, and enemies design ransomware that exploits the logical gaps, physical cracks, digital voids, and the single point of failure in binary computer science to freeze operations. When the logic of the λ-calculus hidesthe implementation details of the latest Turing Machine, golden tokens and distributed function abstractions scientifically prevent all this, but without the λ-calculus, the world sleeps naked with ruthless enemies.

As if this is not bad enough, the binary computer promotes the unelected, centralised, branded superuser as a software dictator, the single-access point of failure to the physical world. The operating system dictates everything, from virtual memory paging to communications, keyboards to computer screens, and computer security. However, the binary instructions remain unregulated at the point of contact, which is how malware starts.

Binary computers can only catch errors using parity bits, encryption and decryption with successful backup images, checksums, cyclic redundancy checks, and error-correcting codes. These methods, including encryption, use extra bits to detect and correct errors during transmission or storage. For example, a Hamming code is an error-correcting code that fixes single-bit errors in a set of data bits. However, undetected software errors and hidden malware are more severe dynamic, computational problems that operate with typed digital information.

It is the nub of the difference between the mechanical and information ages. Binary computers are from the past and cannot detect programming errors because they cannot understand information. When programming began, binary software was considered quickly fixed and always flawless, but in life, it is untrue. Worse still, in cyberspace, good and evil coexist. Outside interests create malware as terrorists breaking into the cockpits of computer science to fly chosen applications into the ground, resembling the software- driven Boeing 737 MAX catastrophes that locked out the pilots as the planes crashed vertically into the ground or the 9/11 terrorists who physically invaded the cockpit and flew into the World Trade Centre, the Pentagon and crashed in Shanksville, PA.

Operating systems rely on the assumption that the software they execute is trustworthy and follows the intended functionality. However, malicious software disguises itself as legitimate programs, exploits system vulnerabilities, and manipulates the superuser privileges and the users to gain direct access to the computer. Operating systems have no way to verify the semantics or the intent of the software they run, nor do they have the means to monitor the behaviour as it occurs. Thus, anomalies and malicious activities are undetected, and malware evades discovery. Neither the binary hardware nor the operating systems can stop these unauthorised and harmful actions on the system or the network once any security system has been penetrated.

Like all dictatorships, the operating systems grow over-centralised, increasingly blind to discontent, and dangerously more dependent on corrupt and untrustworthy bubbles and henchmen attempting to maintain order by increasing authoritarianism. Malware thrives and culminates in a double extortion ransomware attack, the digital equivalent of a revolution that not only encrypts the data after overthrowing the branded superusers in charge but demands additional payment to prevent damaging publications. The attack usurps the superuser and scrambles the boot record and any binary data to freeze everything except a demand for money or unconditional surrender.

The Cold War never fixed the binary computer, so it was never ready for what came next. Everything changed except this centralised architecture when the microprocessor displaced the mainframe. Personal computing and networking exploded, the locked rooms and expert teams vanished, and insecurity surfaced that remains unsolved. The binary computer never matched the science defined by Church and Turing before WW II. It was always scientifically outdated, but binary computers have become a take-it-or-leave-it situation. There is no semantic protection at the coal face of computer science where software drives hardware, malware is undetected, and ransomware thrives with debilitating consequences that AI-enabled network administrators promote to international catastrophes.

Since 2000, exponential growth has taken place with five primary shifts:

1. Cyber threats have become more complex, with attackers using advanced techniques to exploit system and network vulnerabilities.

2. There has been a noticeable increase in the frequency of cyberattacks, affecting businesses, governments, and individuals alike.

3. Cyber threats have evolved, with ransomware, phishing, and state-sponsored attacks growing prevalent.

4. The impact of cyber incidents has grown, with significant financial, operational, and reputational damages incurred by victims.

5. Prestige prevents full reporting as industries and nations strive to protect their state- of-the-art image.

Ransomware has profoundly destroyed the cybersecurity myth like no other form of malware. It clarifies that organisations lack the skills and understanding for essential security work. It is not just a question of training since the Confused Deputy attack is a systemic problem with binary computers that is only solved by removing the superuser. It means things deteriorate, and re-evaluating all alternatives, including solving the flawed binary computer, is urgent. At the same time, getting security right becomes impossible with the spaghetti code consequence of binary computers. To democratize cyberspace demands a cookie-cutter, standardized scientific approach to computation defined by the λ-calculus. The replacement of the binary computer is the only option for the long-term future of cyber society as the nation is placed ever more at risk.

Semantic protection following the λ-calculus is the scientific essential that ensures software is executed consistently with its intended meaning and functionality. Semantic protection relies on mathematical logic and formal methods to verify the properties and behaviour of software and detect and prevent any deviations or anomalies from the expected semantics. Semantic protection can be applied at distinct levels of abstraction, such as source code, intermediate code, binary code, or machine code. Various techniques, like static analysis, dynamic analysis, runtime verification, or proof-carrying code, can also implement semantic protection. Of all these techniques, Capability-Limited-Object- Oriented-Machine-Code offers the best, complete solution because it aligns with the λ-calculus and the golden tokens, providing an open-ended mechanism for security in everlasting cyberspace. Moreover, it is fail-safe because it is an ever-present independent crosscheck performed by a capability navigator next to the code pilot in the cockpit of a Church-Turing computer.

CAPABILITY-LIMITED-OBJECT-ORIENTED-MACHINE-CODE

W hen implemented by machine code, semantic security maximizes system reliability, productivity, and performance. When machine code prevents malware attacks, detects malicious activities, and enforces semantic security policies, the cookie-cutter result is that everyone becomes a good programmer. Moreover, skill shortages disappear, results improve, and productivity increases dramatically.

The Church-Turing Thesis unites logic and physics through symbolic binding. It is a formal system for expressing computation based on function abstraction and application. It allows functions and operators to be symbolic expressions manipulated by rules of substitution and reduction. Unlike binary computers, which store data and programs in physically shared memory modules, the λ-calculus has no notion of memory or state. Instead, it relies on binding, which can associate a name with an object as a networked function abstraction. It supports far more effective concepts than the simple values binary computers offer. It makes a Church-Turing Machine digitally secure, far more potent than binary computers, and forever future-safe throughout cyberspace.

The λ-calculus provides semantic protection against malware attacks by isolating and sandboxing all code as dangerous. For example, running a program we can call P downloaded from the internet requires the program name to exist in the set of names in the namespace we can call N. Thus, a λ-calculus namespace N restricts the available names to those approved by the programmer for an application based on requirements and the need- to-know rules. The function abstractions in the Namespace have a smaller private subset list, which limits the subset of functions.

Thus, semantic security prevents unauthorised access to and manipulation of data and programs. Additionally, encryption protects data and programs from being read or modified without the proper key. Obfuscation hides the structure and logic by transforming them into equivalent but more complex expressions. Finally, verification ensures that programs have the desired properties and behaviours using types and access rights to confirm mathematical logic as a proof system. These checks are performed in parallel by capability-limited symbolic addressing. This hardware technology replaces the centralised mechanics of virtual memory and encapsulates the distributed, dynamically bound laws of the λ- calculus in real time.

The single points of failure in binary computers combined with AI-coordinated ransomware seriously threaten the nation's economy, digital security, and vital infrastructure. It disrupts essential services, compromises sensitive data, and extorts millions of dollars from businesses and individuals. The Center for Strategic and International Studies and McAfee Corp. report that the global cost of cybercrime was estimated at $600 billion in 2017, or 0.8% of global GDP. The US alone suffered losses of $109 billion, or 0.64% of its GDP. Malware also risks national defence, as foreign adversaries use it to spy on, sabotage, or influence military operations and critical infrastructure. Finally, and most importantly, the trusting citizens suffer because they cannot solve these specialised branded troubles and are losing trust in the government and the nation's founding principles.

Foreign attacks on the nation's infrastructure are acts of war. One example is a Big Freeze. An attack by an enemy state intent on crushing democracy. Instead of a slight annual loss of less than 1% of GDP, the Big Freeze is a coordinated international incident. Such planned war attacks are prepared with malware hidden deep in the Homeland, intending to cause the maximum failure—a 100% loss of national capacity for an extended time for nations run by software.

The dominant computing architecture of binary computers is inherently vulnerable to these attacks. The lack of digital security and the single point of failure allows unauthorised access and manipulation of data and programs stored in shared memory modules, causing ransomware. Ransomware prevention and mitigation increases the skilled staff shortages caused by constant vigilance, additional investment, unavoidable weakness, and urgent teamwork among all involved in finding, fixing, and preventing the Big Freeze and lesser catastrophes.

Beyond doubt, the computing paradigm essential for the survival of cyber society in the endless future needs industrial strength. Industrial-Strength-Computer-Science supports software engineering, which can be scientifically depended upon as fail-safe. There are no single points of failure, ransomware is prevented, malware is always detected and prevented, and unfair centralisation, the root cause of digital dictatorship, is replaced by functional distribution following the science of the λ-calculus. Scientifically removing the single point of failure using the λ-calculus creates Industrial-Strength software modularity engineered by calibrated component reliability. Digital privacy now exists automatically, while application and information security are program-controlled by six Church commands used by programmers to navigate a λ-calculus namespace.

Program-controlled digital security combined with symbolic addressing is a game changer, preventing malware and putting programs in control of functional security. It changes the nature of binary machine code, adding the six specialised, program-controlled machine instructions that navigate the namespace web of λ-calculus modularity. Transparently, individual, type-controlled actions are encapsulated by capability-limited context registers. Atomic modularity clarifies digital boundaries and different data types, individual threads of execution enforce privacy and stop insecure sharing, and Capability-Limited-Object-Oriented-Machine-Code harnesses the laws of theoretical mathematics using symbolic names implemented as immutable golden tokens representing interconnected ideas of any type, size, and scope, location, access rights, and complexity.

When software is decomposed as natural atomic functions and assembled as a modular, interconnected application, digital security is program-controlled by a λ-calculus namespace as structured, physically enforced object-oriented software. Program- controlled, type-sensitive digital boundaries protect the content of the individual atomic objects authorised by the assembly, each with an expressive, symbolic name. Digital boundaries exist and are checked by the context registers as the machine code executes, keeping programs on track between the typed digital guard rails of the various context registers.

With a unique name, the object type, assembled size, and related access rights are remembered by the namespace. The unlock instruction retrieves the object's attributes from the namespace and caches them in a context register. The program can now use the content according to the limited access rights authorised by the programmer.

Now, malware is locked out and cannot be authorised or used by a namespace. Moreover, any programming mistake is automatically detected by the typed digital crosschecks of Capability-Limited-Object-Oriented-Machine-Code. Furthermore, the named keys that unlock access rights are the same immutable digital tokens called capability limited addressing. Keys that add encryption and obfuscation if object verification alone is insufficient.

Capability data and binary data are distinctly different. One type is the traditional binary data of 1s and 0s. It can be manipulated and changed using traditional machine code commands within the limited scope of a symbolically named data context instead of any random memory address as in a binary computer. The machine's other data type recognised by the Capability-Limited-Object-Oriented-Machine-Code is an immutable token of an accepted size and format that includes customised access rights. A token is the digital gold of computer science physically protected by the Capability-Limited-Object-Oriented- Machine-Code. The tokens unlock access to individual digital objects using a context register and an unlock instruction.

The digital gold is a qualified, calibrated programmer's private key to control data privacy and information security. Naming programs as protected digital objects creates a calibrated mean time between failures that conveniently identifies the place for software improvement, which is impossible with consolidated, compiled images created for binary computers. This advantage rapidly increases the quality of the Namespace to create flawless software applications. The digital boundaries detect every error and clarify the exact place in the Capability-Limited-Object-Oriented-Machine-Code that attempted to operate out of bounds. Debugging is radically simplified dramatically accelerated, and exhaustive testing can be guaranteed. Trusted software becomes a reality even when developed by an amateur. The democratization of computer science is advantageous for children as well as experts.

COMPUTATIONAL SCIENCE

The history of computer science is summarised below in Table 2, A Recap on the Long History of Computer Science. It covers what, why, and how the Church-Turing Thesis is vital to achieving Industrial-Strength Computer Science. It is never too late to apply science, even at this advanced date. Replacing a poorly engineered solution for the majority is constructive and productive. Democratising cyberspace is good for progress, better for society, and vital for democracy. Binary computers are trapped in a dead-end canyon led there by a dictator, deadly to digital pioneers hoping to find the trail to a democratic cyber society.

The books explain the essential need for computational science as the alternative for a fully engineered, well-calibrated, dependable, and trusted digital future. It explains how this alternative implementation offers an ever-improving foundation for democracy. A democracy defended by cyberspace as nationally engineered function abstractions. This alternative evolves the independent namespace applications on the common AI-powered cyberspace platform. Networked function abstractions are safely engineered and calibrated in depth, breadth, and detail by matching an application as a digital twin scientifically connected to the physical world through the distributed architecture of the λ-calculus. Each Namespace is a scientifically engineered digital implementation of the Church-Turing Thesis, the science of computer science.

The thesis implies that there is no essential difference between what the human mind and machines can compute, given enough

22

time and resources. The focus is not on the computer as a static physical machine but on the dynamic process of logical computation. It is the scientific foundation of computer science and states that a machine can perform any computable function following a set of rules. It has two alternative implementations:

First, it uses the equivalence of Turing machines and recursive functions, which are models of computation based only on procedures statically bound together as mathematical chained functions. Static binding is a physical process that gets increasingly complex as the software grows. It leads to spaghetti code, which is hard to understand, untangle, and costly to maintain.

Second is the equivalence λ-calculus, the model of computation based on functions and abstractions, as the foundation of theoretical mathematical science. The thesis provides a way to formally define the concepts of algorithm, complexity, and decidability. However, in practice, the two alternatives are as different as chalk and cheese: a fragile, dangerous binary computer compared to a scientific, industrial-strength machine.

Period	Development	Impact on the Progress of Society
Antiquity	Birth of Civilisation	The Cellular Personal Abacus, Democratization of Arithmetic, The Silk Road, and Trade instead of barter
Renaissance	The Age of Discovery	The democratisation of religion, to understand the relationship between God, science, the universe, the earth, and the stars.

1614-1800s	Civilised Progress	Science over opinion, Napier's Logarithms, The Slide Rule, the Democratization of Mathematics, and The Industrial Revolution. (Slide rules also created the Atomic Bomb, the Jet Age, and The Moon Race).
1850++	Industrial Revolution	Flawless Machines, The Difference Engine, First Symbolic, Functional Program, Sketch of The Analytical Engine Invented by Charles Babbage, By L. F. Menabrea with notes by the Translator A.D.A. (Augusta, Countess of Lovelace)
1930s	The End of Empires	The Science of Computation, Cryptography, ENIGMA, λ-calculus, Atomic Turing Machine, the Church-Turing Thesis, World War II
1940s	World War II Recovery	The von Neuman Architecture, Binary Computers, Shared memory, Offline compilations, Programming Languages, Monolithically Compiled program images
1950s	The Cold War	Centralised software, Two-level memory, virtual memory, superuser hardware security
1960s	Human Rights	Mainframes business grows, IBM-360, Operating Systems, Monitors, Nobel Prize on DNA, a biological riddle solved.

1970s	Semiconductor Age	Backwards Compatibility, Personal computers, Networking, PP250, Capability-Limited-Object-Oriented-Machine-Code
1980s	Microprocessor Age	The adoption of Personal Computing, Objective-C, The Apple Mac, Graphical User Interface
1990s	The Internet Age	Deployment, Hacking, and Malware all grow
2000s	Digital Dictators	Complexity, Application, Ransomware, corruption, and crime accelerate
2010s	Cyberwar Age	Attacks on global enemies using hacks, tricks, and gimmicks, Growth of ransomware
2020s	Age of Artificial Intelligence	ChatGPT, Superhuman Malware, Multinational Ransomware Attacks, Big Freeze Dry Runs
2030s	The Future	The democratisation of Computers and Cyberspace Church-Turing Computer Science, Fail-safe computers, On-the-spot digital security, Capability-Limited-Object- Oriented-Computers, Industrial-Strength Computer Science, Networked Function Abstractions, End of malware

Table 2, A Recap on the Long History of Computer Science

In the simplest terms, computer science has two sides: a physical implementation side and a logically programmed side. They must work and play together dynamically.

1. The first approach of binary computers is initially straightforward, programmed as simple, statically compiled, sequential procedures. Still, the static physical binding leaves dynamic cracks, gaps, and voids, requiring a centralised digital dictator to connect things dynamically and link to the outside world, the network, and other compilations. As applications and networks increase in scope, size, and number, understanding, programming, debugging, and preventing malware becomes more challenging and complex. It hides untested conditions, leaves unfound bugs, fosters undetected malware, creates new attack vectors, and causes enormous skill shortages as the opaque, centralised physical dictatorship grows and the spaghetti code becomes unstable.

2. The second approach is scientifically driven as a cookie-cutter approach to scalable independent programs. Following the λ-calculus, dynamically bound atomic units are distributed as function abstractions, protected as a private namespace. The atomic structure is secured, and rules never change or grow more complex, whatever happens in the future. Furthermore, the standardised transparent method of λ-calculus abstraction democratises complexity, guarantees industrial strength, and simplifies computer science for all to read and learn as quickly as when at school.

The binary computer uses the first solution but fails to keep software safe and on track on an industrial scale as the spaghetti code and patching grow. Programmable security must be built-in for software to be engineered and kept fail-safe. Machine code has the unutilised potential asthe most potent and rewarding of all programming languages, but only if physics and logic are correctly connected using the cookie-cutter solution of golden tokens with the λ-calculus.

Just six Church commands implement a cookie-cutter solution for the λ-calculus. See Table 3, The Six Church Commands. One Church command exists to unlock functional access to each unique type, the Namespace, a Thread, the in-line Abstractions (Call and Return), every program as an executable block of Capability-Limited-Object-Oriented-Machine- Code, plus digital Objects of all and any type. The cookie-cutter produces scientifically correct results from the input of a golden token. It is far easier to understand than the spaghetti freeform approach of binary machine code because it is atomically standardised, reliable, scalable, open-ended, and secure. Enforcing the laws, the logic of the λ-calculus, and symbolic addressing creates trusted computer science.

3. The freeform spaghetti approach is prone to accidental errors, misunderstood complexity, and undetected malware because it lacks a consistent computational framework for dynamic protection. The λ-calculus has a straightforward hierarchal structure that covers every case. The Capability-Limited-Object-Oriented-Machine-Code places security in the hands of the programmer and the end-user, simplifying complex applications by making software readable, accessible, and democratic.

Anyone familiar with binary computers can learn and understand the six commands. All the baggage of binary computers and spaghetti code is unnecessary, complex, authoritarian, and opaque. It makes every patch hard to fix and even harder to find without creating unwanted side effects, requiring specialised machine code skills.

	Church Command	λ-calculus Action	Access Rights
1	Switch Namespace	Unlock a Namespace Table	Load Namespace Context Register
2	Change Thread	Swap and Suspend Thread	Load Thread and Machine Registers
3	Call Abstraction	Enter Abstract Node	Push Abstraction on Stack
4	Return Result	Return to Prior Abstraction	Pop Abstraction from Stack
5	Execute Code	Unlock Code Block	Load Code Context Register
6	Unlock Objects	Unlock Object	Type Dependent Load Context Register

Table 3, The Six Church Commands

The six cookie-cutter commands are effortless to apply and replace the decades of baggage reinvented too often for branded versions of the binary computer. The better alternative is Industrial-Strength Computer Science following the laws of λ-calculus, binding the logical side to the physical details as a Church-Turing machine for a scientifically safe and secure future. A flawless scientific check and balance creates a reliable, fail-safe computation. Trusted and qualified industrial strength detects semantic errors to withstand worst-case dynamic conditions. Errors are detected on the spot to recalibrate the software reliability of each function, every abstraction, all threads, and different applications as a fully qualified namespace. At the same time, malware interference is locked out of the computational cockpit of computer science by the programmer's control over digital security.

The calibrated MTBF[3] prioritises any weaknesses for improvement. Reinstallation is easy because the offline binary recompilation is no longer mandatory. Capability-Limited- Object-Oriented-Machine-Code is a high-level language, and an online assembly process allows code updates to occur directly after code errors are identified. The speed with which complex applications are integrated using fail-safe machine code is dramatically improved over binary recompilation. Minutes replace hours, hours replace days, days replace weeks, and weeks replace months.

Each golden token is digitally secure, atomically scalable, and network-ready. A real-time, up-to-date measure of MTBF calibrates each function abstraction. Capability-Limited- Object-Oriented-Machine-Code reinforces all. The golden tokens are bejewelled

---

3   Mean Time Between Failure, MTBF is a metric that measures the average time interval between two successive failures of a system or component. It is used to estimate the reliability, and availability of software systems, as well as hardware devices. The higher the MTBF, the more reliable the system is. MTBF can be calculated by dividing the total operating time of a system by the number of failures observed during that time.

with customised rights and signatures of an office. These are the immutable secret keys to unlock only approved namespace objects with designer-engineered access rights— removing any need for the privileged centralised operating system.

On the other hand, binary computers are weak and physically flawed, lacking a logical computational framework and, as a result, an adequate means of digital protection. Bugs and malware corrupt, disrupt and mislead society. Worse still, bugs are only detected at a far higher cost after the event when harm has already spread to the users. Error detection by users instead of by the computer is not science. At the same time, digital dictators increase their authoritarian constraints, attempting to find ways to prevent errors that cannot be seen, thereby extending their authoritarian digital dictatorship and the progress towards Orwellian society. The problem grows from unregulated binary machine code, which is freeform, invasive, and dangerous. When mixed with shared digital memory, hidden input, and output devices, malware can usurp control, kill the superuser, and scramble the system. Accidentally and deliberately, undetected corruption occurs, leaving software decapitated, a frozen computer, days of lost time, and another round of upgrades with additional overheads, Orwellian digital surveillance, and constraints.

Binary machine code only supports procedural programs in shared binary memory, and as everyone knows from personal experience, shared code hides malware, leaving criminals unfound and corruption undetected. Binary computers are enduringly unsafe and digitally vulnerable. Enemies, crooks, hackers, and spies exploit the design flaws, changing the computer from friend to enemy. Malware and program bugs shift the direction and nature of natural computer science away from fail-safe atomic distribution to a centralised digital dictatorship that harms individuals, fragments society, and overrules democracy.

No guard rails exist without the natural logic of the λ-calculus and symbolism dynamically binding programs as logically named functions. Digital corruption is obscured because all that binary computers understand is the difference between zero and one, and the centralised operating system hardware privileges managing virtual memory and hidden input-output devices. None of this is related to the execution point of a failure. The binary compilation is a digital void; the only guard rails are cross-checks added by the programmer or the compiler.

Undetected errors are unsurprising because science abhors a vacuum when something is missing or incorrectly designed. The void exists because von Neumann ignored the λ- calculus. Without this functional modularity enforced by Capability-Limited-Object-Oriented-Machine-Code, binary computers need offline programming languages and centralised, privileged operating systems in a flawed, misdirected, and unscientific attempt to bind and keep programs together correctly, and without the interference of digital terrorists using hidden malware. It is impossible because physical instead of logical binding is shared without the democratic essence of computational privacy. Using a shared binary address allows other procedures to attack the exposed physical memory, input-output hardware system, and every critical detail of the offline compilation. The first-generation design is flawed, like the first generation of steam engines that exploded and killed innocent operators, passengers, and spectators.

But unlike the engineers of that day, computer scientists have, with only the PP250 exception, ignored these threats and risks to individual citizens for a century. The digital void in binary computers is an unregulated gap between the digital compilation and programmed intent lost by the offline compilation. Knowledge and understanding are absent from the binary image malware seeks to fill. Without objective digital boundaries, nothing physical exists to prevent accidental bugs or unregulated downloads, including malware, from taking control. It is proven repeatedly, day after day. In the extreme case of Ransomware, everything digital is frozen by encrypting the operating system, the boot programs, the compiled images, any data, and all the backups held on the disk of a compromised binary computer. It is all the result of missing logic, ignored when John von Neumann abandoned the λ-calculus after World War II.

For society to survive in cyberspace for peaceful future generations, computers must follow science. It is the only guaranteed solution to enemy malware and unwanted dictatorship. The symbols of theoretical mathematics and λ-calculus cannot be ignored. They prevent misunderstanding, undetected errors, outside interference, and silly mistakes.

This framework was proven in the 1970s, 80s, and 90s, as used by the PP250, and explained in Book 1 of this trilogy. Networked function abstractions bound by machine code as reliable computations are the digital twin of the real world. The computer mirrors the world. The λ- calculus aligns the physical to the logical sides of dynamic computation. It is essential. The only way to ensure programs remain safe, secure, and reliable is when a programmer is firmly in charge of digital security by programming with Capability-Limited, Object-Oriented Machine Code.

The λ-calculus also enables computer science to evolve and adapt to new challenges and opportunities, such as artificial intelligence, distributed systems, cryptography, and, one day, quantum computing. By supporting symbolic machine code over binary instructions, the λ-calculus is realised, and computer science avoids the vacuum and fulfils its potential as a scientific discipline.

The Church-Turing Thesis, refined in 1936, hides all physical implementation details from attack, but the teamwork of Alonzo Church and Alan Turing ended before it could be built. So, after World War II, when John von Neumann overstretched Turing's binary computer and ignored the λ-calculus, he broke the mould without any objection from the founders. The λ- calculus hiding all implementation details disappeared, exposing the statically compiled binary image to attack. He wanted to be the leader of this new field first, so he published his idea prematurely, knowing a lack of patent cover would lead to rapid adoption. However, without the λ-calculus, it was an unsound, unscientific shortcut only fit for startup trials and to satisfy von Neumann's ego.

The missing rules became a centralised single point of failure. Digital dictators now increase authoritarian controls, but try as they might, the cracks, gaps, and voids remain. Society, democracy, and civilisation are dangerously vulnerable as digital dictators supported by their operating system henchmen take over cyberspace and rule cybersociety. These outdated computers and corrupt software now rule the world.

For a while, binary computers were successful as a stand-alone mainframe, but they were always locked in a glass room and guarded by a large team of Information Technology experts. The IT experts are only skilled in one of many brands and released versions of centralised operating software running binary computers.

Then, by the 1980s, the microprocessors, as personal computers, bypassed everything needed to keep the software on track as designs were carried forward, and backward compatibility froze meaningful improvements. Personal computing and digital networking created cyberspace but encouraged malware, ransomware, corruption, and crime internationally as a worldwide digital battlefield. The war using complex digital weapons that began as hacks, tricks, and gimmicks now attack global enemies and destroy national independence.

A Big Freeze is the worst result, the ultimate looming threat, the grim reaper of a digital dark age, when critical missions freeze and cybersociety halts from the ultimate coordinated failure. Coordinated failure is a Weapon of Mass Destruction, a global attack. It is the total loss of digital access rights in cyberspace, a Big Freeze. Not for any price will decryption keys be found. Even if they are decrypted forcibly or unrequired, lost backups, delays, and incompatible recoveries discombobulate results. Even experts cannot recover incompatible backups just a day out of date. It took Delta Airlines over a week to recover from the accidental Big Freeze in July 2024, and they faced no insurmountable problems.

The loss of digital reliability, the failure of networked integrity, and the ascendance of digital dictators result from bankrupt binary computers, fractured network infrastructure, flawed centralisation, outdated binary computers, and impossible-to-follow best practices, including compatible backups and workable recovery plans. The Big Freeze stagnates society while the overheads of restoring and sustaining services overwhelm.

Malware, undetected crime, and centralisation guarantee that without the λ-calculus, computer society, democracy, and civilisation can only decline. Increasingly, binary cyberspace is too flawed, unsafe, vulnerable, and complex to maintain. Hacks, malware, crimes, and authoritarian abuses succeed at ever-accelerating rates, driven by the intelligent individuals owning smartphones worldwide to use as a digital trigger in off-the- shelf attacks. Such attacks are already in the works, easily purchased on the dark web, and some are already AI-powered.

Computer scientists must secure the future, adopt symbolic addressing, add back the λ- calculus, and follow the Church-Turing Thesis. Only then will safe and fair science be applied for all, devoid of centralisation, undetected corruption, digital dictators, and criminals. A solution of networked function abstractions secured by the science of the λ- calculus. A future-safe, fail-safe cyberspace for the endless future of national democracies worldwide.

ABSTRACTING DEMOCRACY

Democracy is constantly under threat. It is only a generation away from failure. Dictators are the problem; the world is replete with them in many different shades and with various international and national motives, and binary cyberspace is on their team, leading the attack deep inside democratic society. Thus, this generation must fight to resist dictators and sustain individuality, freedom, equality, and justice in cyberspace as functioning democracies in many different national forms. Unlike dictators, democracy puts the citizens first, but each nation follows a national variation.

For example, the United Kingdom and France are both democratic countries, but they have very different governance systems. Automating these differences subservient to binary dictators cannot satisfy either form of national democracy as expected and required constitutionally. The United Kingdom is a parliamentary constitutional monarchy, while France is a semi-presidential republic.

1. In the United Kingdom, the monarch is the head of state but is limited to ceremonial duties. The Prime Minister holds the executive powers and is answerable to both chambers of Parliament. The British system is called a fusion of powers, where the executive branch is drawn from the legislative branch, which provides checks and balances.

2. In France, the President is the head of state and of the government and is popularly elected. The French system grants executive powers to the President of France. The

President appoints the Prime Minister responsible for naming the cabinet ministers. The French executive branch comprises the President, Prime Minister, and cabinet. Bills must pass through Parliament to become law. The French separation of powers is more defined, with minimal overlap between the branches of government.

The main difference between these and other democratic systems is the power distribution between the branches of government. The United Kingdom has a fusion of powers. In contrast, France has a more defined separation of powers, and every nation has yet another way to distribute power within their society. At the same time, cyberspace envelopes the world with various brands of digital dictatorships, placing international democracy under unseen, undetected, ever-increasing threats.

Indeed, binary cyberspace is the ultimate automation of the deep state, the infrastructure of the unaccountable, unelected bureaucrat, and the handmaiden of the civil service. For this reason, industrial-strength computer science is vital to protect society from government overreach.

Consider the example of Estonia, a country that has embraced digital governance. Estonia provides e-residency and online voting services, showcasing how democratized digital solutions can enhance transparency and citizen participation. However, this digital success also highlights the need for robust cybersecurity to prevent centralised control and deep state manipulation.

Another example is the healthcare system in the United Kingdom, where digital records and automated systems streamline patient care. While these advancements improve efficiency, they also underscore the importance of securing all digital infrastructure against data breaches, ensuring patient data remains private and protected from digital authoritarianism.

How can an industrial democratic nation fully invested in cyberspace and software automation prosper and survive, subservient to branded digital dictators running computer science? Increasingly, the software in cyberspace rules individuals, industries, societies, and nations, but it takes life in the wrong direction. The future of cyberspace cannot be run as centralised dictatorships.

Consider another critical way democracies differ in their voting systems and the methods used to elect their representatives.

1. The United Kingdom uses a first-past-the-post system, where the candidate with the most votes wins a seat in the House of Commons. The party with the most seats forms the government, and that party's leader becomes the Prime Minister. It tends to produce a two-party system and a single-party government, but it can also result in disproportionate representation and wasted votes.

2. France uses a two-round system, where the candidates with the most votes in each district advance to a second round of voting unless one candidate wins more than half of the votes in the first round. The candidate with the most votes in the second round wins a seat in the National Assembly. The party with the most seats forms the government, and the President appoints the Prime Minister from that party. It tends to produce a multi-party system and a coalition government but can also result in strategic voting and runoff fatigue.

Further, a second house of government, known as an upper house, exists in every case. It is a legislative chamber that usually has less power than the lower house but can act as a check and balance on its decisions. The United Kingdom and France have distinct types of second government houses, reflecting their historical and constitutional differences.

1. The United Kingdom has the House of Lords, which consists of about 800 members appointed for life, elected by their peers, or inherited their seats from their ancestors. Some may track back to Runnymede and the Magna Carta in 1215. The House of Lords can review and amend bills passed by the House of Commons but cannot block them indefinitely. The House of Lords also has some judicial functions, such

as hearing appeals from lower courts and acting as the UK's final appeal court. The House of Lords is often criticised for being undemocratic, unrepresentative, and outdated, and there have been various proposals to reform or abolish it.

2. France has the Senate, which consists of 348 members who are elected for six-year terms by indirect universal suffrage. The Senate represents the territorial interests of the French regions, municipalities, and overseas territories. The Senate can review and amend bills passed by the National Assembly but cannot veto them. The Senate also has some special powers, such as initiating constitutional amendments, referring bills to the Constitutional Council, and delaying the declaration of a state of emergency. The Senate is often criticised for being conservative, elitist, and irrelevant, and there have been various proposals to reduce its size or powers.

All these policies and procedures exist in the natural, physical world. But as cyberspace envelopes the world, dangerously exposed binary software automates life. Increasingly, the digital dictatorship that drives binary computer science conflicts with every individual national form of government. Again, for example, in the United States, a Senate of 100 members is elected for six-year terms by direct popular State votes, while in contrast, Russia has the Federation Council, consisting of 170 members appointed for six-year terms by the regional executive and legislative authorities.

However, when abstracted and automated by software in binary cyberspace, these differences are subservient to an unelected digital, industrial dictatorship. This generation's fight for democracy is to remove all forms of unelected, centralised digital power over individuals and to cope with every national difference in detail.

Edger Dijkstra (1930-2002) was a Dutch computer scientist who influenced software as a discipline from both practical and theoretical perspectives. He said, *'The purpose of abstraction is not to be vague, but to create a new semantic level in which one can be absolutely precise.'* In this context, 'absolutely precise' means exact and true to form in every digital detail[4] . He expresses the need for a digital twin as a namespace of comprehensible, tokenised, programmed abstractions without dictatorial operating system interference or any threat or risk from enemy attacks, malware, or even one undetected mistake.

The mere existence of a centralised operating system as an ultimate digital dictatorship prevents Dijkstra's vision. Automating national governments is underway, but only one form works. It is the centralised, procedural, authoritarian form of binary computer surveillance already operational in China and other enemy Orwellian states. The better, nay essential form supporting various independent national governments cannot be created because they are necessarily subservient to a centralised operating system and a digital dictator, all too easily overturned by ransomware. What purpose do the armed forces serve if, one night, enemies crush the nation in cyberspace?

Every form of national government must be as vigorously defended in cyberspace as in the air, on the ground, at sea, and in outer space. The risk of the Big Freeze, or any other WMD attack on this scale, engineered by our international enemies at any cost, must be prevented, and the natural science of the λ-calculus is the future-safe mechanism proved by PP250 to work. Democracy must be abstracted nationally in cyberspace, following each nation's laws and customs. This same principle applies to every function in cyberspace. Individuality is the primary tenant of democracy that promotes freedom, equality, and independent justice. None of this is achievable with centralised binary computers, and consequently, one way or another, democracy is doomed.

The scale of international cyber threats equals those in outer space or other national and civil defence forms. Security in cyberspace is a matter of global and civil defence, including homeland security. The design of cyberspace is no longer a game that is left to industrial dictators using questionable, backwards-compatible motives. The consequence of failure is too significant for the nation and the citizens.

---

4   The right level of abstraction (johndcook.com)

Consider the present situation. Backward compatibility drives digital dictators primarily interested in growing existing market share, including the dictators in China, Russia, North Korea, and Iran, where Big Tech is helping suppression by providing tools and platforms to monitor, censor, and manipulate their citizens. For example, Google is developing a censored version of its search engine for the Chinese market[5]. Project Dragonfly complies with any government regulations on online content to filter out topics on human rights, democracy, and, for China, Tiananmen Square.

Similarly, Facebook is criticised for allowing Russian trolls and bots to spread misinformation and propaganda during the 2016 US presidential election and for blocking the accounts and pages of Iranian dissidents and activists at the request of the Iranian government. Furthermore, Twitter deleted thousands of tweets and accounts that exposed the brutality of the North Korean regime and its nuclear ambitions, allegedly due to pressure from China. Additionally, Amazon has been selling facial recognition software to law enforcement agencies in countries with poor human rights records, including China and Iran.

Facial recognition is used to track and identify any and every citizen and can identify protesters, journalists, and opposition leaders.

Everyone in Big Tech is focused on these dramatic and frightening software improvements, such as building massive data centres to run AI, blockchains, crypto mining, and the like. However, no one is concerned about providing mobile solutions to protect individuals from international criminals and digital dictators. The industry is self-obsessed, racing forward on high-cost inventions, leaving personal computers stuck in the past, using unsafe and outdated architectures and corruptible digital designs invented in the mainframe age, and afraid to risk changes that could disrupt their captive markets.

Even when DARPA organised the CRASH program, it was subverted into a centrally compromised hybrid solution, as reviewed in Book 1. It was largely ignored and never achieved the stated goal of a fresh start. According to the official DARPA website, the CRASH

---

5   Google Slammed by Senators Over Censored China Search Engine (ndtvprofit.com)

(Clean-Slate Design of Resilient, Adaptive, Secure Hosts) program aimed to create new computer systems resistant to cyberattacks and adapting to changing environments. The program ran from 2010 to 2018 with a total budget of $170 million. The program funded several university-led research teams to explore various aspects of secure system design, such as memory management, hardware architecture, code verification, and operating systems. The program also supported the development of prototype systems, such as Morpheus and CHERI, to demonstrate the feasibility and benefits of the clean-slate approach. However, none of the CRASH projects resulted in a commercially viable product or a widespread adoption by the industry or the government.

On the other hand, the US military budget for 2023 was $817 billion, according to the Fiscal 2023 National Defence Authorization Act signed by President Joe Biden. It involved $177 billion for the Army, $194 billion for the Air Force, including the Space Force, and $231 billion for the Navy and Marine Corps. The issue of a cyber-secure civil democracy was not considered.

Still, suppose one includes the FBI, CIA, NSC, and, appropriately, Homeland Security funding. More than sufficient funds exist to invest in research and improved computers for civil defence, following science as the unquestionable next step and avoiding the industrial dictators who distorted the CRASH program. The President's Fiscal Year 2023 Budget for the Department of Homeland Security (DHS) is $97.3 billion, representing an increase of $6.5 billion from the Fiscal Year 2022 President's Budget[6] . This funding reflects a continued commitment to homeland security and the American public. Yet, the issues raised by this trilogy are never discussed, even when brought to the attention of DARPA as a CRASH proposal.

President Eisenhower's warning about the industrial military triangle was a farewell address he delivered on January 17, 1961, in which he cautioned the American public about the dangers of the military-industrial complex's excessive and unwarranted influence on the government and society. He argued that the close relationship

---

6   Workforce Development | Homeland Security (dhs.gov)

between the armed forces, the defence industry, and the political leadership could threaten democracy, civil liberties, and peace. He urged the citizens to be vigilant and informed and to balance the need for security with the need for progress and freedom.

The significant problem with the industrial-military triangle is that it works as a powerful lobby of vested interests that influence political decision-making and public opinion, regardless of the needs or the consequences for democracy and human rights. Digital dictators amplify this worry by using their control over binary computers and cyberspace to manipulate information, spread propaganda, censor dissent, survey citizens, and even undermine elections. They and others exploit the vulnerabilities of centralised, outdated systems to spy, launch attacks, sabotage infrastructure, steal data, disrupt services, and rewrite history.

By doing so, Big Tech becomes an industrial arm of the Deep State, resisting improvements and efficiency while eroding trust and confidence in democratic institutions and freedom. It creates a climate of fear and insecurity, justifying more centralised authoritarianism spilling from cyberspace into society. Digital dictators not only threaten civil society but also hold ultimate power in cyberspace, where World War Three is fought, national security is hinged, and the sovereignty of the United States and its allies depends.

This trilogy addresses the gap in civil defence after the failure of the CRASH program and shows why and how it is vital to protect democracy in cyberspace. It is imperative to change course and invest in a second scientific generation of fail-safe personal computers for civil defence. A Dream Machine that protects civilians in cyberspace from corruption and dictatorship to guarantee the integrity and resilience of digital democracy in the USA and its allies. It is once again a question of national defence against foreign and domestic enemies.

Funding for a new generation of safe computers that use symbolic instead of physical addressing is a tiny percentage of the numbers. The United States federal budget for the fiscal year 2023 totalled $6.134 trillion in expenditures, representing approximately 22.8% of the GDP. This budget was enacted as part of the Consolidated

Appropriations Act, 2023, a $1.7 trillion omnibus spending bill signed by President Joe Biden on December 29, 2022, or approximately 1.22 million staff years. This calculation assumes an average annual salary of $50,000 per staff member, which is a rough estimate.

The cost of developing a redesigned PP250, already proven as a starter kit for Homeland Security, would need about 300 staff years if it is run as an independent task on a black site beyond the influence of lobbies, about one-thousandth of the 2023 Federal Budget. A billion-dollar investment that preserves civil rights and protects the future of cybersociety, the USA, freedom, equality, justice, and the American way of life.

It is urgent because, unfortunately, the rise of binary computers has gone too far as a WMD in enemy hands. DARPA and CRASH failed, and the personal computer remains firmly stuck in the past and cannot be trusted. Democracy suffers while dictatorships and our enemies prosper. The centralised binary computers are too easily abused and misused; worse still, these unfair computers have split the national will to resist.

Few individuals understand that the nation must fight as hard for democracy today as those willing to shed their blood yesterday. The war zone may be in cyberspace, but the fight is for individuals who prize our freedom and the freedom of future generations. However, centralisation's power crushes individuals' will to resist, rooted in hypnotic applications and hidden digital corruption that allows dictators to prosper. This downhill path is driven by industrial greed, fuelled by backwards-compatible, outdated computers and unpunished criminals.

The digital dictators of the computer industry, DARPA, and the CRASH program have all failed to advance, so private investment with Homeland Security must work outside Eisenhower's industrial military triangle must step up. For the reasons explained, the President should issue an Executive Order for Homeland Security's mission to lead the charge and fund the forgotten side of computer science to preserve the Constitution and guarantee our civil rights in cyberspace. It is not an option. It is a question of survival, as inscribed on the Lincoln Memorial. It is a national priority for 'we the people.' Personal computers must catch up with the threats to the Constitutional Republic by removing the centralised powers of a digital dictatorship. Instead, the freedom, equality, and justice of networked function abstractions are democratic solutions for the people. Equally importantly, it is also run by the people through the golden tokens that restore individual power to the hands of citizens as a working, balanced, democratic cyber society for the Information Age.

CYBERSOCIETY

The vision of Alonzo Church and Alan Turing in 1936 was purely scientific but, therefore, automatically atomic and distributed. Alonzo researched the perfection of the natural logic of computation as atomic function abstractions, and his student Turing understood an atomic digital machine as the engine of functional computation. In this model, Turing's implementation details are hidden and guarded by data-tight, function-tight abstractions that symbolically use the essential rules of theoretical science. Sadly, their partnership ended just before World War II, and the idea was unfinished. So, a decade later, John von Neumann took a different stab at a solution.

He knew both Church and Turing and met with Turing to discuss implementation details before Turing returned to England, but now he wanted to be first and saw his chance. He discarded Alonzo's λ-calculus solution without review or objection. John von Neumann failed to appreciate the critical importance of the λ-calculus regarding dynamic binding, symbolic addressing, and function abstraction. He naively overstretched the atomic Turing machine and broke the scientific mould that hides the implementation within the λ-calculus. It was the dying days of the Industrial Age, and no one understood the digital future or how the λ-calculus and the perfected science supported dynamic atomic computation.

Centralisation is the driving force behind today's computer science. This backwards- compatible, unscientific attitude also undermined DARPA's CRASH program. When hybridised by the establishment, CRASH failed to produce a clean start and commercial results. Next time, this cannot be allowed.

Soon after the partnership between Alan Turing and Alonzo Church dissolved, the war in Europe began. Turing returned to lead the Hut 8[7] project that shortened the war. Explaining the λ-calculus as the science of computation in nature remained misunderstood for another half a century until the PP250 was designed. Instead, von Neuman overstretched the Turing Machine into a proprietary binary computer, and the simplified, unscientific, one-sided, limited physical idea as a stand-alone computer took off.

The λ-calculus remained ignored until 1969 when the PP250 engineering team searched for a fail-safe solution of shared networked software for global computer-controlled phone networks and put the two halves of the Church-Turing Thesis back together. I can say firsthand that the ideas were driven by a fear of malware transmitted easily by the shared hardware in networked binary computers. The PP250 achieved Industrial Strength in

Computer Science and proved that Capability-Limited, Object-Oriented Machine Code could deliver decades of unfailingly engineered software reliability. It is only possible when all traces of the centralised binary computer industry are purged from the next generation of computers through Capability-Limited-Object-Oriented-Machine-Code.

Every brand of binary computer for the personal use of desktop and mobile users remains stuck in the past, bound to the ageing physical world of the Industrial Revolution by backwards compatibility. There are too many digital flaws, and all are vulnerable. The design cannot

---

7   Hut 8 was a section in the Government Code, and Cypher School (GC&CS) at Bletchley Park (the British World War II codebreaking station, located in Buckinghamshire) tasked with solving German naval (Kriegsmarine) Enigma messages. The section was led in WORLD WARII by Alan Turing.

be engineered or defended, the software is unavoidably opaque and silently hacked, new software is impossible to test exhaustively, crimes and authoritarian abuse are systemic, and society is turning to fragmented digital dictatorships.

Life has dramatically changed because of computer science and programmed software. It is no longer just a physical world run by nature superimposed by civilisations. Cyberspace envelopes the natural world as an abstract medium increasingly run by AI. In the abstract world of the endless future, information is the king. Survival depends on accepting a future of digitally hardened, logically named function abstractions as researched and resolved by Alonzo Church, pioneered and proven not just for standalone computers but for the full scope of cyberspace by PP250 using the λ-calculus.

Cyberspace exists far beyond the traditions of a mechanical world except for one metric: component reliability. Only the science of λ-calculus abstractions as modular functions can be calibrated and qualified this way. The golden tokens and the digital ironwork of the PP250 produced dramatic results—Industrial-Strength Computer Science to span the world. Software reliability exceeded hardware reliability. As a telecommunications switch, the PP250 software lasts longer than the hardware, potentially forever, like Ada's Bernoulli code and the mathematics in a schoolroom textbook.

A civilisation cannot survive using compiled, consolidated, centralised, fractured, unfairly privileged, outdated binary computers. They freely grant unchecked powers and share unguarded physical access rights created by self-interested monopolies, generously gifted to system administrators, spies, crooks, and enemies. These brands of Trojan Horses are used by hackers, thieves, spies, enemies, and even democratic governments to steal, survey, spy, invade the privacy, and overturn the hard-won democratic freedoms of every innocent citizen. As the future arrives, the end-game catastrophe unfolds. Using the binary computer is like bringing a knife to a global gunfight.

Digital dictatorship is already in charge in China, Russia, North Korea, and Iran, and inevitably, the centralised dictatorial global suppliers have put democracies on notice. The end games of cybersociety run this way: branded, fragmented, identical, centralised digital dictatorships fighting over international markets cannot support the diversity of international democratic nations unless they, too, become dictatorships. It is an ominous threat to the values and freedoms of democratic societies, which depend on binary computers for survival and prosperity. Competition was lost due to increased entry costs and resistance to change.

Even if AI never reaches the point of singularity, it already exceeds humans' memory and instant recall capacities on any chosen subject. Subjects include programming skills in any desired language. With this ability, the branded binary computers guarantee global failure. The supply chains that feed industrial society do not need to fail at home. They are quickly attacked overseas.

For example, a national grid collapse in unstable nations like Nigeria threatens oil. Likewise, terrorists in Aden threaten transportation routes while enemies launch ransomware worldwide. Binary computers run these critical supply chains, feeding metals like iron, copper, aluminium, and steel to run factories that manufacture machinery, vehicles, buildings, infrastructure, and weapons. Minerals, like coal, uranium, lithium, and rare earth elements, generate energy, power electronics, and produce batteries. Chemicals, such as fertilisers, pesticides, plastics, and pharmaceuticals, are needed to enhance agriculture, protect health, and create consumer goods. Timber makes paper, furniture, and construction materials. Water purification and supply are essentials for human survival, agriculture, industry, and sanitation.

The consequences of digital failure impact everyone everywhere. Many countries, especially those that depend on imported resources, have weak digital infrastructure. The World Bank says Nigeria has one of the lowest electricity access rates in the world, with only 60% of the population connected to the national grid and an average of four hours of power supply per day. Nigeria is only one example. The inferior quality and reliability of electricity and digital services is a significant obstacle to economic development and social welfare and a source of political unrest that ferments terrorism and environmental pollution.

Add to all this the risks of a Big Freeze. The current binary computer system running resources like the global supply chain is prone to failure and manipulation not just by malicious actors, terrorists, rival states, and governments everywhere but also by mistakes in software upgrades, as happened in July 2024. AI only amplifies these problems to cause widespread, harder-to-unravel disruption and damage internationally, leading to further disasters, conflicts, and humanitarian crises.

The only way to limit these scenarios and support democracy worldwide is to follow science and apply the Church-Turing Thesis and the λ-calculus. The PP250 proved how fail-safe, future-safe, digitally secure, democratic computer software works reliably without unfair centralised privileges. The scientific solution of λ-calculus works, but more importantly, it prevents dictatorial forms of government from taking over. Furthermore, it enables individual nations to abstract and control their destiny, protect themselves according to their specific laws, customs, and traditions from external interference, and avoid subservience to the unelected central powers of digital empires.

The risk of power grid failures internationally is pessimistic alarmist, but the facts and direction of binary computers are not. Digital threats evolve as software is so frequently updated, and only one mistake can cause a catastrophe. AI malware makes everything worse by amplifying problems that already exist. The trilogy explains how the science of λ- calculussolves these scenarios by referencing how the PP250 overcame the same technical challenges. Implementing this change is a political and social challenge, but the alternative is unacceptable. It is the Manhattan Project 2.0, but it is necessary again, and this time, it is inaction that leads to the loss of life and an international catastrophe.

The combination of AI malware, binary flaws, and skilled staff shortages is unsustainable worldwide. For this reason alone, dramatic improvements in digital transparency are required. To guarantee the survival of the USA as leader of the democratic world, AI-driven dictatorship and the collapse of international society must be avoided. It must be guaranteed by engineers like all other life-supporting infrastructure projects and not left to chance as in a binary computer. Software must be scientifically engineered using calibrated, measured, qualified MTBF.

Once modular software is scientifically engineered, the age of branded binary computers ends as we quickly enter the Information Age using open competition with the far better Church-Turing alternative. All it takes is an affordable investment by a concerned private investor in free speech and government efficiency to jumpstart a new semiconductor computer using the λ-calculus and Capability-Limited-Object-Oriented-Machine-Code.

DEMOCRATIC CYBERSPACE

Preserving democracy in cyberspace is critical for AI-enabled cyber society because science is the only way it can be guaranteed. It means that the age of binary computers must end and be replaced by flawless computer science. It is no longer the option it once was when computers began. Fail-safe and future-safe computer science is grounded on the Church-Turing Thesis and uses the λ-calculus. It is sustained by Capability-Limited-Object- Oriented-Machine-Code, which protects software and society democratically, scientifically, uniformly, and safely.

Building ground-up computer science from theoretical mathematics automatically upholds the laws of computational science atomically, privately, and democratically. The free and fair incremental power is safely distributed to society by elected individuals. Immutable, golden tokens reinforce each citizen's individuality as a democracy in cyberspace. Individually, nations can protect their form of elected power from digital dictatorship, corruption, and crime without outside interference or centralised digital dictators.

Alonzo Church scouted the path, and Alan Turing, in 1936, when Alonzo revealed the λ- calculus. His atomic science works equally, correctly, and safely for everyone without the centralised branded advantages created by the digital dictators for their operating system henchmen. There is no centralised, dictatorial operating system with dangerous special opaque powers and the everlasting threat of ransomware when mathematical science is followed.

Furthermore, the science of λ-calculus adds the power of functional programming to create transparent, readable, comprehensible, and powerful machine code. Nations and citizens are freed from centralised oppression and opaque complexity, and anyone can learn to program symbolically to create prosperous, independent, grounded cyber nations. In this new world of genuine computer science, individuals chart their fates secure from foreign interference. It is the scientific path not taken when John von Neumann abandoned the flawless science of the λ-calculus for a deadly shortcut.

Golden digital tokens are immutable digital secrets that distribute power incrementally according to local instead of global policies. It is a sharp contrast to the centralized dictatorships of the binary computer that prevent local alternatives and undermine national democracy. The golden tokensabstract every detail hidden by a symbolic name to an object- oriented class, a functional code block, a thread of computation, some binary data or another namespace located locally or remotely.

The classes link and cluster the functional hierarchy in need-to-know, nodal relationships, a hierarchy of organised digital function abstractions that operate safely. The Namespace define applications as just another networked function abstraction. The reduction of the application carries the instance variables of a computation in a thread to the selected path through the Namespace. The thread traces the dynamic path of each computational step to a result.

A Namespace is a blueprint for a dynamic digital species with an engineered, functional role in cyberspace. It has coherent DNA engineered by the many dimensions of namespace hierarchies, defined by functional nodes and local lists of golden tokens. It is organized into functional, need-to-know relationships as a working digital species with a family tree for incremental evolution and golden tokens for active navigation. The hierarchies securely lock out malware and corruption.

Cyberspace is no longer a corrupt form of centralized dictatorship but a cooperating collection of independent applications. Each abstraction is free and equal, where the independent hardware of

Capability-Limited-Object-Oriented-Machine-Code enforces digital justice. Application programmers use these trusted rules to distribute power independently and fairly through the golden tokens and capability-limited addressing. Power is transferred incrementally as functions in an application hierarchy up to individual users motivated and empowered to preserve their security.

In addition, the known advantages of functional programming now exist in machine code, and unlike compiled images trapped by the operating system, they stretch network-wide. A λ-calculus model of computation implemented in machine code gains all this additional power without any overhead or baggage and with the vital addition of global reach. A digital twin of nature where the abstractions act as the digital genes of a dynamic species, enforcing the DNA of the Namespace as a network-wide computation as needed for the PP250 control of international phone calls. The immutable tokens dynamically express the DNA brought to life as one specific instance at a time by parallel execution threads as dynamic λ-calculus computations. It is the ultimate future-safe form of fail-safe cyberspace. When tokens and abstractions define digital power in computer science, power is distributed according to need instead of shared by default as in a binary computer. There cannot be a single point of failure when using a Church-Turing Machine. The λ-calculus and Capability-Limited-Object-Oriented-Machine-Code solve the problems transparently with simplicity.

The mechanics of sacred, immutable golden tokens as authority to act through access rights is critical to understanding the history of civilisation and the Church-Turing Machine. Unique tokens grant owners power through restricted access rights. These rights can also be revoked by design. Typically, in a democracy, after an election, or by an owner of the abstraction. The incremental and private distribution of digital power is a digital twin of democracy. It is a dramatic contrast to the branded operating systems and hidden privileges of an unelected digital dictatorship created by binary computers that crush individuality, freedom, and democracy.

The centralized operating system acts as a digital henchman, like Barons in the Middle Ages who ruled their peasants as farm animals on behalf of the crown. The dictatorial suppliers of binary computers grant the henchmen unlimited digital powers to control their markets. Also, they collude with national governments and dominant semiconductor suppliers, leaving no room for fresh start competition or individual dissent.

Citizens are peasants of cyberspace, forced to comply with unreasonable rules they cannot understand that pay homage to the supplier. Consequently, the shift to dictatorship accelerates and becomes unstoppable as the point of singularity approaches. Binary computers are flawed, vulnerable, dangerous, and oppressive. They already have the power to undermine democracy and incrementally increase this power in a false claim to prevent corruption but to maximize their control over the global market. It is uncivilized and in direct opposition to the needs of any democracy.

Unless the Big Freeze comes first, democracy is overruled by brands of unelected digital dictatorships enforced by the centralized operating systems of binary computers. The wise solution is to switch away and replace the ultimate threats with Church-Turing Machines, following the ideas implemented by PP250. It leads to a Dream Machine that is vital for the scientific progress of global cyberspace, functional digital democracy, the science of the λ- calculus, and the everlasting protective ring around global cyber civilization. No alternatives exist because nothing else is scientifically guaranteed. It is unreasonable to do otherwise when cyberspace, as a global platform, controls the eternal future of civilization.

THE DREAM MACHINE

Symbolic machine code directly executes point-to-point, right across the surface of cyberspace, unconstrained by physical limitations and unencumbered by centralization. The golden tokens of capability-limited addressing express the science of ideas as a future- safe, fail-safe Dream Machine vital for the prosperous progress of civilization. The tokens could contact distant stars if humanity ever gets that far. Doubtless, communication delay remains a problem, but it is relieved by caching read-only information, leaving only variables to exchange in real-time. The golden tokens have the power of leavers, shifting computer science into the endless future and releasing new levels of simplified fail-safe programmed abstraction and functional networks. Abstractions accessed by the universal cookie-cutter of λ-calculus democratized computer science for anyone to become an expert.

It resolves the skill shortage caused by the opaque complexity, unwarranted overheads, and authoritarian baggage created by the unscientific centralized software of binary computers. The Dream Machine is founded on the λ-calculus, the Church-Turing Thesis, and Capability- Limited-Object-Oriented-Machine-Code. Adding high-level, symbolic tokens to machine code creates an application-oriented namespace for every problem—the PP250 controlled telecommunication objects and dynamic call structures as digital twins of the global phone network and the dynamic call paths.

As a point of reference, the complete Capability-Limited-Object-Oriented-Machine-Code, as the PP250 instruction set, is linked below[8] . It combines Turing's standard imperative binary commands in any RISC machine encapsulated by six Church Instructions. The result replaces page-based virtual memory with symbolic capability pointers instead of shared physical addresses. The hardware baggage of linear memory addressing is replaced by programmer-controlled symbolically named golden tokens. The golden tokens are immutable capability pointers. This change is a like-for-like indirection that trades page- based virtual memory inherited from the Cold War stand-alone mainframes at an equivalent cost and performance but with dramatic advantages.

No price can fully value secure, functional programming inherited by future generations. The golden tokens unlock the full power of transparent computer science through the λ-calculus. Church-Turing Machines leave behind the Industrial Revolution and the purely physical world, carrying the nation into the endless Information Age future of abstract but digitally hardened computer science. The earlier books explain the advantages of high-level machine code as a readable application-oriented language with unmatched functionality, power, performance, security, transparency, comprehension, and operational efficiency.

The abstraction of data types, structures, algorithms, and applications as unified and consistent computations transcends the limitations of stand-alone binary computers, centralized operating systems, and compiled software images. It creates abstract executions that survive, like the theoretical mathematics Ada Lovelace used, for generations on end that can run directly on upgraded hardware because the standard is set by the science of the λ-calculus, not a

---

8   The PP250 Instruction set is found here https://drive.google.com/file/d/1EUcG7mTtdko1Kc9Q_PwGG0LiHwLBxHwP/view

particular brand or year of manufacture. The λ- calculus works like the mind, independent of physical details. Irrespective of particulars, computer science can flourish in ways we have yet to understand without the deadly centralised operating system.

The Dream Machine of symbolic computing is the ultimate form of function abstraction. It allows lay citizens and computer scientists to focus on the essence of their problems or areas of research and interest. Without understanding every detail, the lay majority can appreciate the computational logic and avoid the implementation details.

Artificial Intelligence and every other advanced subject, from cryptography to blockchains, used symbolism to achieve the recent strides. All these progressive steps improve the software's nature and functionality, but the most significant gains remain in symbolic machine code, which must replace the binary machine code. Capability-Limited-Object- Oriented-Machine-Code is the most promising, underrecognized application of symbolic computing. So far, all advances remain trapped on flawed binary computers with decades of unnecessary branded baggage and pioneering struggle to understand and overcome.

The Dream Machine heralds a new computer paradigm that dramatically outperforms binary computations in every critical way while democratising and securing the platform for future generations. These machines, prototyped by PP250, apply and follow the Church-Turing thesis that states that any computable function can be expressed and evaluated using λ- calculus, the formal system of logic invented by Alonzo Church. It is the foundation of functional programming, a change in thinking that treats computation as evaluating mathematical functions where all ideas are expressed and accessed symbolically as in the human mind, rather than manipulating physical states, as in a binary computer.

Functional programming has many advantages over imperative programming. It makes programs concise, elegant, modular, and reliable. See Table 4 Summary of Functional Programming Code Advantages. These advantages are most potent when implemented in machine code, the most significant level of computer science, using Capability-Limited- Object-Oriented-Machine-Code.

Concept	Description
Composition	Meld functions together, constructing intricate functions from basic ones without intermediate steps or additional variables.
Currying	Converts a function with multiple arguments into a series of functions, each with a single argument
Comprehension	Symbolic names enhance readability and understanding.
Higher order	Accept and return other functions, promoting modular design, and managing structural intricacy.
Lazy evaluation	Allows actions to be evaluated when needed, not before, improving performance by avoiding unnecessary activity and covering infinite data structures and streams
Optimizations	Logic, self-tests, automatic debugging, and error detection improved performance by memorising reused functions and parallelization.
Reduction	Applies a function to each element in a collection and combines the results into a single value, allowing parallel and distributed processing of data sets
Reuse	Enhances modularity and the ability to reuse code
Recursion	Allows the definition of functions in terms of themselves, using a base case and a recursive step to express complex algorithms concisely and elegantly
Security	Typed modularity prevents malware and makes programs readable and reasonable.
Transparency	The result depends on its arguments, not external state or side effects.

Table 4 Summary of Functional Programming Code Advantages

These features are all characteristics of the Dream Machine using Capability-Limited- Object-Oriented-Machine-Code, a change in thinking for the future using functional programming for the never-ending benefit of civilized society. Binary computers rely on low- level implementation details, mutable states, and side effects. Unavoidably, these peculiar mechanisms result in undetected digital crimes, malware, and increased authoritarian centralization. On the other hand, a Dream Machine offers functional programming. It allows amateurs, beginners, and anyone of any skill level to learn to write high-performance Capability-Limited-Object-Oriented-Machine-Code. The Dream Machine is designed to guarantee that every program is one hundred per cent fail-safe and non-interfering while virtualizing the logic of human cognition. It democratizes computers by hiding the complexity of today's opaque binary computer.

Like the PP250, the Dream Machine implements the λ-calculus directly through the hardware, using a novel design to combine parallel processing, distributed memory, networking, and self-repair. An arrangement that engineers software applications with decades of fail-safe fault tolerance. The Dream Machine proves more. Consider, for example, executing the dream of Ada Lovelace by running and debugging her Bernoulli code in a Mathematical Namespace.

Ada's machine code was written two hundred years ago for Charles Babbage's unfinished analytical engine. Running for the first time on a Church-Turing Machine proves the scientific magic of Capability-Limited-Object-Oriented-Machine-Code and the incredible productivity gains achieved by Industrial-Strength Computer Science with a software life cycle as long as any physical wonder of the world.

Indeed, other programs written in a functional language, like Haskell, Lisp, or Scheme, can also run directly without a compilation or interpretation when assembled using a language- oriented namespace on a Dream Machine using Capability-Limited-Object-Oriented- Machine-Code. Programming with symbolic names to define logical expressions is no more complex than the ones learned at school.

The dream goes further by testing, generating, and optimizing machine code, using the techniques of meta-programming, partial evaluation, and super compilation to learn to reason and create.

The simplification of computers democratizes next-generation programming using the λ-calculus for its elegance as the foundation of mathematics and functional programming secured by fail-safe machine code as flawless private threads of computation.

The first critical step in the right direction must focus on mobile and personal computers as a defensive tool for humanity. It avoids reworking any data centres. The data centres are run by industry with large IT staff in locked buildings like the mainframe age. The Church- Turing/Dream machine protects and enhances citizens' lives throughout the Information Age. Moreover, it simplifies access to the complex services offered by data centres when single machine code statements can use golden tokens to fetch results from complex and expensive services in the cloud, including the technology changes needed for AI and quantum computing.

THE PROCESS OF EVOLUTION

The first two books, 'Civilizing Cyberspace,', and 'The Fate of AI Society' cover the flaws of binary computers and the criminal nature of the dystopian future the nation can expect. The centralized vulnerabilities that empower digital corruption, cybercrime, cyberwar, and cyber surveillance by digital society's privileged sections are explained. The books introduce the 'Dream Machine'—a scientific alternative that, like PP250, follows the Church-Turing Thesis. The Dream Machine redefines the future by achieving Charles Babbage's dream of flawless computer science and Ada Lovelace's dream of cyberspace as a universal tool of humanity. To date, this better alternative is suppressed and obstructed by collusion between suppliers and governments, who benefit from centralized controls and digital dictatorship at the expense of individual freedom, equality, and speedy justice in a binary- controlled cyber society that works against the US Constitution.

Volume One explains how the PP250 integrated Capability-Limited-Object-Oriented- Machine-Code using the six specialized instructions to enforce the λ-calculus laws. It explains the Church-Turing Thesis as a theorem that encapsulates and hides the binary details of Alan Turing's atomic (unstretched) binary computer, hidden within the dynamic boundaries of function abstractions defined by the λ-calculus. Alan proposed the Turing Machine directly responding to Alonzo Church, his tutor, after understanding the λ-calculus. His atomic machine is the perfect idea for a digital λ-engine of the λ-calculus.

Encapsulating Turing's digital computational machine as the hidden engine of Alonzo's λ- calculus conceals all binary and other implementation details, protecting the machinery from attack. Dangerously exposed details attacked by binary machine code include the shared memory page registers and the centralized superuser. The single points of failure include computer administrator accounts and theft of credentials easily used by ransomware. Such flaws can freeze the system, install undetected malware, hide digital corruption, and perform silent crimes, from annoying hacks to full encryption.

However, the science of computer science is decentralized and distributed, centred on the λ-calculus as the unchallenged foundation of mathematics and the theory of computation, implemented as Capability-Limited Object-Oriented Machine Code. Nature is built on cellular distribution. Atomic science avoids any need for centralized branded dictatorships. Instead, power is distributed atomically, incrementally, equally, fairly, and independently. Copied to cyberspace, the digital twins of national democracy can now exist without the override of a digital dictator. It creates a judicious digital foundation where nations, industries, and individuals can all prosper simultaneously, independently, and cooperatively as the abstraction of civilization without an overriding dictatorial bias.

The earlier books explain how fate brought on this dilemma and the scientific history of computers that began with the private, cellular wooden Abacus. This atomic cellular copy of natural life advanced with Napier's logarithmic scale and the multi-function slide rule that removed the need to remember the details of every mathematical function. Then, in the 1840s, at the height of the Industrial Revolution, Charles Babbage created his 'Thinking Machines', and Ada Lovelace wrote the first program. They did not end the mechanical age but opened the door to programmable functional computers. Ada programmed Babbage's machine using theoretical mathematics and, in 1843, published her notes explaining her vision of computer science.[9] A vision that saw into the future far beyond Babbage's numeric focus.

---

9   Ada added her ideas as Notes A-G to her translation Sketch of The Analytical Engine (fourmilab.ch) by Luigi Federico Menabrea, an Italian military engineer, and mathematician known for his explanation of the Analytical Engine.

The binary computer is unlike all historical examples. It is a machine code puzzle, not a fail- safe machine like a Church-Turing machine. The science is unsound because it lacks any means of atomic function abstraction. For example, the Abacus abstracts the human hand. It took the object-oriented machine code of the PP250 to square the circle of Ada's visions, going well beyond Babbage's programmable Analytical Engine and the first programmed function abstraction of the Bernoulli series. Adding the six Church machine instructions encapsulates an atomic digital machine as the hidden engine of λ-calculus functions. The books explain how machine code abstraction creates flawless functional computers without the threat of malware, ransomware, centralized single points of failure, unelected branded dictators, and undetected digital crimes.

When Ada Lovelace wrote the first-ever program as the function abstraction of the Bernoulli series, she dreamed about program-controlled music, art, and literature. She predated Objective-C's achievements in Steve Jobs' hands by over a century and a half. While Babbage coded programs to prove his work, Ada's vision went far beyond his, as she explained in her published notes and letters. All Ada used was Babbage's symbolic mathematical machine code. There was no compiler, no operating system, just symbolic programming, the language of mathematics. She extrapolated this idea to the arts well beyond science.

The idea was successfully copied by PP250 in 1972. Dramatically, her ideas still ring true because they pass the test of time using science that has the power to last forever. Theoretical Mathematics

---

Menabrea attended Babbage's seminar at the University of Turin in 1840 where Babbage unveiled his plans for the Analytical Engine. Subsequently, Menabrea published an account of the lecture in French in the Bibliothèque Universelle de Genève in October of 1842. The work is recognized as the first description of a computer and is an important milestone in the history of computing. At the request of Charles Wheatstone, a family friend, and co-inventor, Ada Lovelace translated Menabrea's work into English and included extensive notes including the first published algorithm a Bernoully series abstraction she programmed using Babbage's mathematical machine code that allowed her to pass variables, and functional expressions as in the λ- calculus, and with functional programming.

works endlessly, so her program makes sense two hundred years later and, like a schoolbook, remains for eternity. Moreover, she grasped how symbolic abstraction applies equally to the arts, such as synthetic music, computer-generated pictures, and AI literature.

After one and a half centuries, Steve Jobs confirmed her vision with the Mac and Objective-

C. This powerful new object-oriented technology also rebuilt Apple Computer from bankruptcy. However, unlike PP250, Apple and all other attempts to capitalize on this technology use compilers and retain a central superuser operating system. Jobs had no choice because the Capability-Limited-Object-Oriented-Machine-Code was still under patent protection.

The additional security and power of Capability-Limited-Object-Oriented-Machine-Code is irresistible. If readers remain unconvinced, imagine the productivity gain when computer machine code is flawlessly failsafe, atomic, and networked as reusable function abstractions with the same life span of centuries, like Ada's example. Further, the danger of centralization vanishes. When scientifically expressed machine code remains unpatched for generations, the opaque black spot of binary computers is enlightened.

Machine code could be as easy to read as a schoolbook, understood clearly, reasoned about, cross-checked, exhaustively tested, and engineered to remain fail-safe under worst- case conditions for generations. The λ-calculus simplifies computer science by replacing decades of baggage, including debilitating centralized failure points, dictatorial operating systems, offline compilers, monolithic binary compilations, and networked administrator's single points of failure. Only then can Industrial-Strength Computer Science be achieved and the Information Age begin earnestly.

As the final instalment, this book examines the advantages of Industrial-Strength Computer Science, the cost, the end game, the need for government leadership, and the critical steps to preserve freedom, individual rights, and the US Constitution. It is the scientific path to everlasting democratic cyberspace. It offers low-cost, long-lived, highly productive, functional software digitally secured by Capability-Limited-Object-Oriented-Machine-Code.

Capability-Limited-Object-Oriented-Machine-Code is as robust, reliable, and enduring as Babbage's mechanical Difference Engine. The MTBF of exhaustively tested modular software is calibrated and can be engineered. Readable, transparent machine code replaces the opaque baggage created by and for binary computers and their digital dictators.

Symbolic, scientific machine code that has the potential to last forever and, once functionally tested, never needs a patch.

This software is read like a professor's chalkboard. Functional transparency with calibrated reliability is the true definition of Industrial Strength Computer Science. Modular software with accurately calculated and constantly updated Mean Time Between Failure rates that identify specific failures and prioritise incremental, guarded improvements. Failure rates that exceed the best hardware. When ransomware is locked out, reliability reaches beyond decades instead of a few weeks. Monthly software upgrades are made unnecessary, and function improvements are made incrementally.

The modular software enforced atomically by Capability-Limited-Object-Oriented- Machine-Code achieves this sophisticated intensity as Industrial Strength Computer Science. It ensures secure, flawless, future-proof, and fail-safe digital computations for experts and novices alike, and this point is the most important to grasp. Democratization of cyberspace means anyone from children to the elderly can program and experiment without risk and without mastering the opaque software and in-comprehendible best practices that make binary computers so hard to work with.

Amateur programmers, school children, retirees, experts, and nations can coexist on their terms, which Capability-Limited-Object-Oriented-Machine-Code faithfully guards and reliably guarantees. It purifies the whole meaning of democratic cybersociety as free, independent citizens and nations democratically share the common platform called cyberspace. Each actor is an individual instance of a digitally secure Namespace, for example, a living digital twin of a citizen in a national society.

Think of Namespace as a secure cybersuit that is environmentally engineered to allow citizens to navigate dangerous international cyberspace safely as a dynamic instance of a complex digital species. They are empowered to use the full functionality and safely survive in an AI-enabled cyber society. In this democratic cyberspace, power is incremental and decentralized, distributed to citizens functionally by private golden tokens. Hardware centralization and digital dictatorship are removed, malware is locked out, and ransomware becomes impossible because there are no single points of failure. Because Capability- Limited-Object-Oriented-Machine-Code applies the Church-Turing Thesis, the λ-calculus guarantees computer software, applied as a cookie-cutter science, and cyberspace cannot threaten citizens, democracy, or civilization.

While the earlier books, 'Civilizing Cyberspace', and 'The Fate of AI Society' expose the international dangers and an unavoidable dystopian future, this book explains the way forward. The path not taken after World War II. The Scientific Path to Industrial-Strength Computer Science and the Information Age. It argues for the US Government to reclaim computer science from Digital Dictators and criminals. It is a cause as important as the Revolutionary War, the Civil War, and all World Wars. To scientifically upgrade cyberspace and use democratic function abstractions for national independence and avoid Orwellian dictatorship.

Even the earliest computer, the Abacus, worked using an atomic abstraction of the human hand and a threaded chain of private atomic numbers. The power to prosper individually, transparently, and democratically sparked trade, prosperity, and civilization, but centralization is opaque, oppressive, dangerous, strange, and understood by no one. The branded result leads to opaque centralization, digital dictatorship, raw industrial power, common theft, and selfish greed that fragments and undermines civil society. Stable software that lasts and avoids incremental upgrades engineered to sustain market dictatorship instead of the scientific progress of civilization.

The first attempt, the PP250, was delivered in 1972, and at that time, it cost eight million pounds Sterling. It took less than three hundred staff years of engineering effort from mid- 1969 to 1972 when it went to market. It proved successful for digital communication from the 1970s to 1990s, serving the British Army in the First Gulf War. Still, without a silicon foundry, it could not compete with Intel microprocessors, and ever since, the cost of semiconductor technology prevents outside competition.

However, as explained, when redesigned, sponsored and distributed by Homeland Security to immunize and preserve the constitutional democracy of the tenets of the USA. It must be outside the existing computer industrial-military framework—an offsite 'tiger team' funded as was done for COVID-19 vaccines. The cost is a tiny fraction of government spending, far less than 1% of GDP, needed to prevent a national disaster and WW III loss to the international enemies.

The result of this next-generation, scientifically motivated redesign would radically change the future. Productivity accelerates because software development is simplified, patched upgrades are avoided, life cycles are extended, and maintenance on the binary baggage of decades is avoided. Building digital twins as complex networked abstractions is transparently and directly achieved by readable machine code, making progress faster across a broad civilian front where citizens directly interact with computer science. Every citizen remains secure from crime and interference while learning to enjoy programming cyberspace as quickly as civilization took to the Abacus and the slide rule, with the same unexpected global expansion in ideas and civilization. Importantly, democratic nations are saved from the international, undetected, dictatorial threats that circle the world of binary cyberspace and can build their national digital twins of democracy without fear or favour.

Book 1 'Civilizing Cyberspace' explains how this mess began and the technology that solves the problem. Book 2, 'The Fate of AI Society', reasons this change is the only way to protect nations, individuals, freedom, and democracy. Given the acceleration threats in centralized binary computers and the emergence of superhuman AI malware, it illustrates the moral and political implications of inaction.

The danger of deliberate AI breakout by an enemy state targeting the USA and industrial democracy is horrendous. AI malware and the Big Freeze are as infectious and more disastrous than the COVID-19 pandemic shutdown in 2019, while the solution is not so quickly resolved. Redeploying cyberspace with a new generation of computers and software is not as easy as vaccinating the population.

Vaccinating computer science against malware requires digital genes of Capability-Limited- Object-Oriented-Machine-Code to exist to purge malware, corruption, and dictators. In addition, every centralized operating system must be repackaged as an abstraction to offer software backward compatibility. It allows all existing applications to migrate without a total rewrite while achieving the immediate protection of Industrial-Strength Computer Science. The functional abstraction of centralized services reduces the cost and time needed to avoid an Orwellian endgame and a Big Freeze.

Securely decentralized authority using immutable golden tokens and networked function abstractions are data-tight and function-tight. The improvements pay for themselves from the savings on maintenance alone. Distributing democratic powers safely, incrementally, and ultimately into the human hands of citizens. It is the only way to preserve and protect democracy. Over time, developing dependable network function abstractions is a national advancement towards a resilient international digital democracy.

Decentralization defends the future from dictatorship and individuals from criminals. Confidential data and privileged information are safeguarded within digital vaults and secured using encrypted access tokens. They unlock the immutable digital ironwork of cyber security. Networked abstractions implemented by Church-Turing machines empower individuals in flawless, future-safe cyberspace, while Industrial Strength Computer Science resolves the risk of malware, cybercrime, and default dictatorship.

This concluding volume reemphasizes the role of scientific digital boundaries enforced by Capability Limited, Object-Oriented Machine Code to build and maintain cyberspace as Industrial-Strength Computer Science. This future safe technology guarantees personal liberty while upholding democracy and protecting various cultures independently within Cyberspace. It counteracts the Orwellian regimes rooted in adversarial dictatorial enemy nations and the danger of the USA abandoning the US Constitution and becoming another digital dictatorship. The book tackles the transformation, weighing the cost against the consequences of inaction, and elaborates on the significant benefits of secure, functional machine code. It explains the absolute urgency for action as international threats grow and the digital WMD looms over the nation.

SURVIVAL

How can democracy survive and thrive in a digital age driven unscientifically by centralized corruption and digital dictators who encircle the world? How can we protect the individual rights and freedoms of citizens democratically from the digital dictators and the cybercrimes of spies and thieves? How do we stop national decay through international cyberwars and slavery to some superhuman digital intelligence when the point of singularity is reached, AI breaks out, and takes control? How can we design and implement the ultimate Dream Machine for future-safe cyberspace that solves these problems while remaining secure, efficient, and intelligent? How can we reflect the ideals, values, and principles of every democratic society and national culture? These are the critical questions the trilogy tries to unravel.

History shows that the freeform spaghetti code of binary computers repeatedly fails in too many undetected, tragic ways, disorganized, and threatened by operating systems, administrators with superuser powers, and unsafe single points of failure. It motivates programming languages and compilers to limit but not eliminate these breakdowns. It also led to monolithic binary compilations introducing new risks from centralized failures. Flawless binary software is impossible. The spaghetti effect cannot be untangled, no matter how hard we try. However, the solution is avoided by the symbolic names and dynamic binding rules of the λ-calculus.

The core problem is the lack of a sound computational model and the substitution of centralized power. The binary computer has no feedback loop and is unable to self-correct. Centralized operating systems run binary compilation using superuser privileges and incorrectly assume that everything functions perfectly at the point of contact between hardware and software. It blindly follows the classic formula of a dictator's bubble. From the era of Roman rule to medieval monarchs and nobles, through the age of European Empires, and including the Cold War, autocratic governance consistently leads to failure. However, binary cyberspace changes government powers, allowing surveillance and subversion powered by unelected digital privileges. Computers spy, crush freedom, dominate society, and rewrite history. Orwellian society is in the making and getting closer to abandoning the US Constitution and the Bill of Rights and replacing democracy.

The root cause is systemic. Binary cyberspace is centralized and authoritarian by the nature of binary computers using privileged unelected operating systems, the baronial henchmen of digital dictators. After decades of failed attempts to patch over these problems, the unexpected still occurs, and disaster strikes again. These disasters include a frozen

industrial society caused by the Blue Screen of Death.[10] At best, the tricks for a brand are tolerated by learning to work around one set of frustrations as design constraints. However, this does not solve the problem of centralized administrators and single points of failure. One mistake and the Blue Screen of Death strikes again. In a network, it could stop a nation or even the world in its tracks. Worse still, the cure is horrific, requiring extra authoritarian constraints to prevent unexpected hostility.

---

10   The blue screen of death also known as BSoD, blue screen error, but known officially as a Stop Error is a critical error screen displayed by Microsoft Windows. It indicates a system crash, in which the operating system reaches a critical condition, and can no longer operate safely. Every centralized computer has such a case.

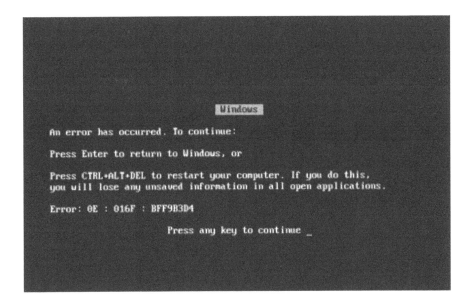

Figure 2 The Blue Screen of Death

From Caligula to Stalin and others, dictators stay in power through paid henchmen, and binary computers are no different. It limits the binary computer to, at best, self-serving dictatorships. It is not as it could be, and it must be as a global platform for fair international competition. Cyberspace must be scientifically fair and engineered as a dependable, trusted global platform that humanity can confidently use to prosper and grow as progressive, civilized, independent and very different democratic nationsfor the rest of time. As a claimed science, no other form of public engineering allows unpredictable calamities and total collapse as an unguided, unguarded WMD.

The problem is the centralized nature of software engineering. Natural science can always be reliably engineered, but not so for the binary computer. Ask why, and the answer is centralization. Dictatorial centralization is the problem civilization has fought since history began. Dictatorial unreliability cannot be quantified. There is no way to calculate the MTBF of software functions for a binary computer because the individual components are a collective compilation as one binary image randomly attacked by outsiders. When patching became a monthly upgrade, the actual performance was masked and remains unknown. The industry hides behind shared corruption and universally blames the user when something goes wrong.

So, unreliability is masked by monthly downloads that introduce new risks like faulty versions but allow suppliers to duck and push responsibility onto users by claiming, after any failure, that the user is to blame. They failed to install or follow some unreasonable, just published, new best practices. In truth, the suppliers fail to engineer computers scientifically.

However, there is hope. It exists in Capability-Limited-Object-Oriented-Machine-Code. The PP250 already proved how this level of applied engineering solves all the unacceptable binary conditions, with the additional advantages of networked functional programming. Functional programs add exceptional powers over procedural programs. See Table 4 Summary of Functional Programming Code Advantages. Capability-Limited-Object- Oriented-Machine-Code supports network-wide functional programming in machine code by following the science in the Church-Turing Thesis and using the λ-calculus to frame the science of flawless functional programming. This scientific alternative is founded on distributed, MTBF-calibrated modularity instead of centralized single points of failure.

Modularity and distribution combine as the alternative scientific framework of computer science. This framework applies capability-enforced limitations that prevent malware, dictatorship, and single points of failure. Secret golden pointers and the digital ironwork of capability context registers enforce the functional limitations in cellular chains of atomic object-oriented cells. Power in nature is distributed this way, theoretical mathematics is taught this way, and a democratic society functions similarly through the symbols and logos of power assigned to each elected office. Alonzo Church defined universal mathematics this same way through the λ-calculus.

Centralization guarantees lost freedom, the fear of constant disruption, and eventual dictatorship. Binary computers are on this unnatural path of dictatorship and crime. These two threats, crime and dictatorship, are the systemic threats of dictatorship and forecast the enslaved Orwellian future of humanity in the age of cyberspace.

Industry and government profit from centralization, so the distributed solution is ignored. Thus, we, the people, must speak out. The government holds the purse strings and the executive power to force the change. The scientific and humanitarian justifications are overwhelming, but no commercial progress has been made despite the DARPA-CRASH program. Even so, the change must come, or unelected dictators and the unnamed tyrants of Eisenhower's industrial-military alliance take over computer science, and democracy drowns in a sea of digital dictators, global crimes, and international wars in cyberspace that spill into the physical world.

All this tragedy is avoided when the science of λ-calculus applies. Democratic computer science solves the problem. Industrial-Strength Computer Science is achieved this way. It is a crucial step because it is the only way to civilize cyberspace, the subject of Book One. 'The Civilization of Cyberspace' explains the dilemma and how a world of progressive individuals and democratic cyber societies digitally collided with the dark side of humanity. The unacceptable consequences are international digital warfare, synchronized ransomware, the Big Freeze as over-complex administration fails, and recurring digital catastrophes that lead society to ever-increasing dictatorship.

WORLD WAR III

W orld War III has already begun, and the systemic weakness of binary computers and related opaque problematic software makes digital survival a national priority. The nation must demand digitally armoured software for personal use built into smartphones, laptops, and PCs. The digital armour must have the industrial strength to keep individual citizens safe from all foreign and domestic enemies. Cyberspace as an international battlefield defaults to a Federal Government responsibility, and they must step up.

The computer industry is disinterested because they quash competition and make too much money from their captive global markets, selling their addictive dictatorial software and outdated, backwards-compatible binary computers. At the same time, the deep state, in the form of the industrial military triangle, and other government bureaucrats oppose any change. They are devotees of centralized, top-down command and control. They led this approach after World War II and throughout the Cold War. Finally, their hidden powers subverted the DARPA-CRASH program to retain backwards compatibility and centralized operating systems.

The present suppliers remain stuck in the past, and the road to national disaster seems inevitable. Only the federal government has the power and the responsibility to fix this national stalemate. Binary computers are a pandemic—a WMD in enemy hands, both foreign and domestic. The funds required for the best alternative are a fraction of the cost of a new tank, a fighter jet, or a drone, and far less than the Naval Warship, far less than another carrier fleet, but the threat to the nation from cyberspace is real, ever-present, and ominous.

It could be treated at warp speed like the COVID-19 pandemic—government-funded, protected from internal subversion, reporting to Homeland Security, and initially distributed freely, like the COVID-19 vaccine. Multiple vaccine versions from at least two significant semiconductor suppliers, ARM and AMD, are government-inspired, following the COVID-19 example. Homeland Security should be responsible for following the Church-Turing Thesis using only the λ-calculus as the cookie-cutter factory of distributed reliable software. Backwards compatibility must be limited to software abstraction only.

Industrial Strength Computer Science is not a new idea. It refers to the prior era of physical machines engineered to benefit and not harm. It echoes Ada Lovelace's vision of a future where fail-safe abstractions are the bedrock for a thriving, democratic society, fostering an unbounded horizon. WW III challenges her vision. It shatters her dream and the American Dream. Binary cyberspace is built for dictatorships where China, Russia, Iran, and North Korea are the victors on the binary battlegrounds of cyberspace.

Yet, pursuing individual freedom in Cyberspace is paramount for the survival of democracy, a cause for which countless sacrifices have been made. As a bastion of liberty, the beacon of hope, and an undisputed technology leader of cyberspace, America plays a pivotal role in creating the future as in the past, in the ongoing quest for individual autonomy. It is incumbent upon America to face this challenge against a tide of digital tyranny and to uphold its commitment to the global cause of freedom. It is a national responsibility chiselled on the walls of national monuments as America's solemn duty to all humanity. The dream of progress and liberty cannot be extinguished.

Industrial Strength Computer Science began when the Abacus democratized arithmetic. It cannot die with the binary computer. It was law throughout the age of physical machines to 'do no harm.'

Only the atomic bomb came close to an international threat through mutual destruction. The new threat of binary cyberspace is so addictive that we have, like other addicts, lost our collective minds. Cyberspace is so mighty that no one can escape the grip of digital dictators.

The world's destiny is different. It must remain the American dream coloured in cyberspace by Ada Lovelace when she envisioned a world of abstractions on any and every subject that uniformly powers flawless cyber society. WW III cannot be allowed to destroy these dreams. The enemy dictators are the only winners in binary cyberspace, but the cause of freedom is too important. America, as the beacon of freedom, must act. It is vital for the future of civilization and the ideals of individual freedom and happiness. As in the prior world wars, America always stands and saves the world from dictatorship. It is America's gift to humanity enshrined in the Constitution.

So, this trilogy calls for further action that guarantees the decentralisation of software as calibrated Industrial-Strength Computer Science. Modular digital objects, each one having a calibrated mean time between failure of decades.[11] It is the dream of flawless democratic cyberspace, even if it requires a Manhattan Project 2.0, first seeded by a COVID 2.0 pandemic response to win World War III in cyberspace, not just by patching code but by fighting to change the course of history, as America has always done, not for themselves but for civilization, and humanity.

Fighting World War III with binary computers, the dream becomes a nightmare. Moreover, the blood shed by our ancestors was wasted. Democracy, the US Constitution, and the Bill of Rights are lost forever as power continues to move from citizens to unelected digital dictators.

The fight for this generation is once again the fight for the survival of the American Dream. As before, the dark forces of humanity cannot win. It is a fight for the profound survival of the words in

---

11   The time can range from between 100,000 hours to 1 million hours or more where there are 8760 hours in a year.

the US Constitution and the Bill of Rights[12]. It is a technological fight on who decides how computer science evolves. It is not fought on landing fields or beaches but on the surface of computer science, where the forces of binary cyberspace rage. The defensive weapons in this fight are fail-safe symbolic instructions, the immutable golden tokens, and the digital ironwork of capability-limited programmed abstraction. The science of computing, the λ-calculus, and Theoretical Mathematics are the red lines enemies cannot cross. Binary computers crossed these red lines decades ago and now empower our enemies deep inside the homeland. These one-sided computers gave the enemy the upper hand and abandoned the high ground, while ignorance, indifference, and addiction continued to stop a defensive response.

The reason is a paradigm change in warfare. Computer science is abstract—the science of ideas, concepts, and reason. Abstractions grow in the mind. Translating ideas and human thoughts to reality is an act of mechanical or digital computation. Computation is dynamic, as in a machine, not static. This machine converts ideas into action on the very surface of computer science. It is the practical, scientific place to solve software reliability problems and the only place where World War III can be won.

The physical binding of binary computers is static; thus, digital moving parts of the machine are exposed to interference. By dislocating the dynamic mechanisms between a compiler, the operating system, software loaders, and the programmer, the superimposed dynamic abstractions trip and fall on the uneven digital surface of gaps, cracks, and voids.

However, these ideas of the mind are solved by symbols. Symbols that name and represent functions. Names and expressions frame the dynamics of λ-calculus function abstractions. Theoretical

---

12   The Bill of Rights is the first 10 Amendments to the Constitution. It spells out Americans' rights in relation to their government. It guarantees civil rights, and liberties to the individual—like freedom of speech, press, and religion. It sets rules for due process of law, and reserves all powers not delegated to the Federal Government to the people or the States., and it specifies that "the enumeration in the Constitution, of certain rights, shall not be construed to deny or disparage others retained by the people."

Mathematics forged this path where expressions of equality can be thoroughly checked using pen and paper. One sees these expressions on chalkboards worldwide as students at schools and universities learn symbolic programming taught as 'Math.' See Figure 3, Math at School is Machine Code for the Mind.

Ada Lovelace used these same mathematical expressions in 1843 to program Babbage's Thinking Machine, and likewise, the PP250 programs coded a secure global telecommunication application that reached around the world. When implemented this way, World War III can be won. Capability-Limited Object-Oriented Machine Code is the scientific solution to prevent undetected binary attacks where each named object is a digital fortress in cyberspace and, simultaneously, a fail-safe digital twin of the real world.

Machine code is where to implement the scientific solution for program-controlled virtualization with digital security to win WW III. It could not happen after hardware-defined virtual memory froze software as sequential physical procedures instead of named, networked function abstractions. Virtual memory diverted research on software to create an all-powerful, almighty central operating system. However, the goal of computer science is much simpler, as expressed by Alonzo Church and the λ-calculus. Meanwhile, von Neumann's cutoff still blocks the development of distributed software abstractions in machine code.

On the other hand, the PP250 leads to a Dream Machine, a Church-Turing Computer that encourages progress. Using this fact to maximum advantage, the migration plan to this second generation of democratic computer architectures starts by abstracting the widespread examples of binary computers, including the function abstraction of virtual memory and operating systems. Instead of hardware page registers, software capability registers are used. Existing applications running as binary compilations can now migrate without code changes when the first Dream Machines are available.

Figure 3, Math at School is Machine Code for the Mind

This alternative form of programmed backwards compatibility is harnessed to forward scientific progress. The existing applications benefit from digital security. The nation avoids the Big Freeze and digital dictatorship, and the industry develops more complex, higher quality, fail-safe global applications with dramatic cost savings, time, and extended program life cycles. Industrial-strength Computer Science is designed to win WW III, again a war of ideals between dictators and democracy fought in cyberspace.

The ideas of the mind are reproduced reliably when objects of the imagination are Alonzo Church's function abstractions that the λ-calculus can faithfully compute, matching form and function to the thought process. The Abacus, the first such machine for computation, obeys this defining rule of the Church-Turing Thesis as an array of human hands, each able to reliably count from zero to nine. The cellular computation is executed as atomic decimal numbers using four finger beads and a thumb bead on an individual rail. This private tool is inherently safe from spies and outside interference, and it is the same with the individual threads computed by the λ-calculus.

The λ-calculustranslates each named abstraction to the world of programmed computation. The PP250 used this ability built into Capability-Limited-Object-Oriented-Machine-Code to implement each design faithfully. This flawless, faithful ability to engineer software reliably and to programmatically secure function abstractions is vital for the survival of national forms of a democratic society—different national applications distributed equally and fairly throughout interactive cyberspace. The λ-calculus works globally as distributed software, previously proven by international global telecommunications, the audio forerunner of digital Cyberspace. Now, it is needed universally for every application to survive World War III.

Unlike opaque and fragile binary machine code, capability-limited, object-oriented machine code is transparent, digitally unbreakable, readable, self-explanatory, naturally distributed, digitally secure, and fail-safe. Therefore, it is not critical to obfuscate. Instead, each λ- calculus Namespace evolves as a problem-oriented high-level language and IDE assembler[13]. The built-in hardware error detection capability provides debugging on a full- time basis, finding flaws through the fail-safe machine code. Identification is immediate on the first encounter, and a correction is made instantly, shortening the debugging window by months just by removing the offline recompilation.

The named tokens clarify each program statement, as shown in Equation 1, Symbolic machine code Using Capability-Limited-Object-Oriented-Statement for Telecoms, and everything is simplified and democratized as a problem-oriented namespace. Each application has a personal namespace that acts as a digital environmental space suit to navigate cyberspace safely using only the approved golden tokens. When computers are democratized, machine code becomes transparent, and everyone can program safe, high- level statements that solve their specific problems without the opaque, misleading baggage invented in the long-gone early years of binary computers and stand-alone mainframes.

From a survival perspective, WW III must protect democracy. Individuality is the key to democratic government, and centralized dictatorship is the enemy. The thread-based symbolic addressing is

---

13   Integrated development environments are designed to maximize programmer productivity. IDEs present a single way in which development is done. This program provides features for authoring, modifying, assembling, deploying, and debugging software.

like the Abacus and the slide rule: personal, private, and secure instead of public, shared, and vulnerable. The sound implementation of privacy prevents outside interference while detecting programming bugs and locking out malware.

The simple laws of λ-calculus substitution, recursion, lazy evaluation, and immutability encapsulate everything binary. Just six λ-calculus, or Church Instructions, make this possible and replace all the baggage of backward compatibility developed since World War II. Instead of a centralized, privileged operating system and offline compiled images, function abstractions exist for thread synchronization, resource management, device drivers, and other system functions that run within a thread without requiring any hardware- defined superuser. Instead, each abstraction has a private list of golden tokens sufficient for the supported functions of the abstraction.

The six 'Church instructions' programmatically control digital security by unlocking the approved access rights using the immutable secret tokens in a private list that control the λ- calculus execution of an abstraction in each Thread in a Namespace. The function abstractions are linked on a need-to-know basis as a digital skeleton for a dynamic species. The tokens are private keys that unlock gates to local or networked function abstractions and any other authorized object from within the digital Namespace.

The namespace stores the golden tokens as local assess rights in lists for each nodal abstraction in the networked skeleton, translating each symbolic name to the approved implementation. It might be anywhere in cyberspace, local or remote, and it might be anything: a downloaded program, a remote or local abstraction, some remote digital resource, another namespace, or a new idea implemented by a quantum computer in the future. Symbols allow Cyberspace to support open-ended developments like the most innovative human mind and advanced industrial developments.

Translating ideas and things into an object-oriented namespace of digital abstractions creates an in-depth and in-detail digital twin of the idea or the thing. More importantly, the twin executes on the digital surface of the computer as a reflection of flawless science. There are no gaps, cracks or voids between the idea or the thing and the digital implementation. The λ-calculus creates this digital reality as the computation occurs at the point of contact between logic and physics, on the digital surface, at the computational moment when and where electrical energy is expended. It is the only place and time where flawless computer science can be forged with the ability to withstand wicked enemies willing to stop at nothing to create unexpected attacks.

The Capability-Limited-Object-Oriented-Machine-Code atomically automatically acts as a hardware shell protecting each symbolic name as a data and function-tight digital object unfolding like a flower. It leaves no room for undetected mistakes or outside interference, any undetected program bugs, or malware interference. All errors are found on the spot by the fail-safe instructions and caught before any digital harm occurs.

Thus, every machine instruction, including the RISC function (the updated Turing commands) and the Church functions, are engineered to remain fail-safe and programmatically control security. Furthermore, any aborted instruction is caught by the fail-safe recovery mechanism that dynamically updates the log, resolves and restarts the error, and recalculates the MTBF of the objects involved.

Indeed, any theory of computation is missing from the binary computer. The machine code has no such rules to obey. They operate physically, sharing a binary computer's physical objects without the rules dictating the science of ideas. The only guard rails protect the centralized dictator, and nothing exists to keep programs on track or provide a safety net when malware strikes. Indeed, no errors are detected whenever hackers, spies, thieves, or enemies attack. Each programmed step is blindly assumed to work as expected, safely, and correctly, but binary commands are not fail-safe; worse, outside interference, dynamic errors, programmed bugs, and programmed malware cannot be detected.

World War III is lost unless computer science fights back. But binary computers are like a box of loose parts without the life cycle rules of a machine. It makes unexpected corruption easy by using one wrong command hidden in any sequential procedure. Neither the centralised operating system nor an offline compiler can catch these bugs or outside interference. The solution is logically fragmented, making it impossible to engineer a data- tight and function-tight solution. Crooks, spies, thieves, enemies, and stupid internal mistakes occur without a response. The root cause remains unfound, and the corruption is hidden and ignored until it is too late to be fixed and saved in a backup, making recovery after a Big Freeze hard, if not impossible.

Some undetected attacks are so dangerous that they kidnap the centralized operating system, encrypt the digital configuration as a 'Ransomware' attack, and demand substantial Bitcoin payments to restore service through a decryption key. It is a short step for an enemy to synchronise this attack into a national disaster as the Big Freeze, an unrecoverable version of the CrowdStrike calamity of June 19th, 2024.

Ransomware attacks the most prominent single point of failure, the centralized dictatorial operating system in charge of all operational activity. Centralization is the mistake that makes the operating system the enemy. In enemy hands, weapons of war are hidden, ready for a global attack. When it becomes a Big Freeze, it shuts down the nation overnight.

Undeniably, it is only a question of the time and effort our enemies are willing to spend to win WW III.

If it can happen, the only uncertainty is when. Indeed, enemies are planting seeds for a debilitating Big Freeze in binary cyberspace. As binary computers automate the world, they risk a total collapse when the Big Freeze occurs. Trade routes halt, markets stop working, the dollar collapses, and individuals die. It cannot be doubted or ignored; we live on the brink of an international catastrophe more severe and more devastating than either the atomic bomb or COVID-19. The binary computer as unsafe cyberspace is a weapon of mass destruction, a WMD already in the hands of the enemy.

The only hope to survive WWIII is to remove the risk of the single point of failure in binary computers. The ultimate threat of a Big Freeze and Blue Screen events is to end the mainframe age and update the digital computer. The hardware must catch up with software and detect digital threats on the working surface of computer science.

Computer hardware using Capability-Limited, Object-Oriented Machine Code operates better than high-level programming languages by cutting out all the binary baggage invented over decades and placing software security and information privacy in the hands of programmers and citizens.

The winning formula for WW III is software distribution by adding the six Church instructions and the golden tokens. However, the λ-calculus encapsulates and controls security for both the code and the atomic Turing machine, just as Church and Turing intended in 1936. It puts the programmer in charge of digital security details, which are then inherited by users using the tokens they inherit to govern the functionality of their applications—the evident, immutable, object-oriented, capability-limited access rights act as digital gold. Like gold in the natural world, They are things of value. The immutable golden digital tokens define the structural digital power of the DNA as a skeleton of programmed applications, controlling natural movement simultaneously with security. The immutable digital keys unlock programmer-controlled security as access rights to function abstractions. The function abstractions equate to data-tight, function-tight symbols in the λ-calculus.

These modular digital objects are executed on the surface of computer science, adding scientific theory to digital cyberspace. When objects have an unchanging meaning represented by an immutable digital token, they can be translated by a namespace to locate the object in global cyberspace.

The three critical laws of the λ-calculus explained in Book 1, 'Civilizing Cyberspace, the Fight for Digital Democracy,' operate as a Church-Turing machine. The computer performs fail- safe instructions that prevent hacking, malware, and cybercrimes. The flawlessly fail-safe mechanisms only use type-safe, data-tight, function-tight named digital objects as λ-calculus function abstractions without the baggage of operating systems, offline compilations, and dangerous centralized privileges.

Instead of relying on exposed, shared physical addresses, centralized binary memory, and dictatorial operating systems, the science of the λ-calculus is enforced by machine code and capability-limited symbolic addressing. As defined by Alonzo Church, Turing's doctoral tutor, the λ-calculus is far better than the shortcut John von Neumann proclaimed, and the industry has followed ever since World War II.

THE λ-CALCULUS AND FUNCTION ABSTRACTION

S ymbolic computing is used indirectly by procedural programs, every programming language, AI, blockchains, mathematics, cryptography, financial modelling, and every software application. Symbolic computing copies the cognitive process of the mind, but when implemented indirectly, it is inefficient and unreliable. It is exemplified by binary computers requiring a programming language compiler and a dangerously privileged central operating system. They are still subverted by malware and overturned by ransomware, creating staff shortages, high maintenance and support costs, and lost opportunities.

As the scientific alternative, a Church-Turing Computer implements symbolism as fail-safe machine instructions directly on the surface of computer science. Removing all the baggage of centralization maximizes functional power and performance while guaranteeing digital reliability to the universal limit across digital cyberspace. Symbolic addressing mimics the theoretical foundations of mathematics and logic by employing the λ-calculus as a better way to program computer science. Software is more natural, comprehensible, directly readable, and powerful as function abstractions governed by the λ-calculus.

Symbolic computing is also the solution to software security, individual computational privacy, modularity, and, thus, most importantly, quantified, calibrated software reliability. Capability-limited addressing and object-oriented machine code provide the golden tokens, the application skeleton, and the digital ironwork to hold it all in place. The networked function abstractions provide the muscle power to create a secure creature with a backbone, a dynamic skeleton, organs, and the muscles to prosper, evolve, and survive in hostile cyberspace.

The decentralized, distributed creatures are engineered as digital machines with a dynamic framework for applications to thrive. This securely programmed cyberspace is democratic, equal, accessible, and comprehendible to all. Digital crime is detected and prevented democratically and scientifically. Justice is speedy, independent, and fair, administered scientifically and neutrally by the separate mechanisms of Alonzo Church and the λ- calculus through the type-limited digital boundaries of symbolic modularity enforced by capability-limited addressing.

As explained in the first book, the PP250 programmed complexity in the same straightforward way Ada Lovelace resolved her Bernoulli abstraction using fail-safe, readable machine instructions. Each instruction references named capabilities, the function abstractions of the λ-calculus, a mathematical system that expresses computation rules elegantly. Alonzo Church invented it in the 1930s to study the foundations of mathematics and computability, but it was ignored in the race to build computers after the war.

The λ-calculus has two main components: terms and rules. Both are represented symbolically in all forms of theoretical mathematics. Terms represent functions, variables, or applications of functions to arguments. Rules govern how terms are transformed, simplified, or evaluated. The λ-calculus models a computable function as an algorithm. In other words, it is a program of symbols bound together dynamically, as taught to mathematics students everywhere.

The λ-calculus is the basis of functional programming languages, like Haskell, Lisp, and Scheme, and the capability-limited, object-oriented machine code developed for the PP250. These alternatives use symbols for function abstraction as first-class values, used as arguments or a result of a function, stored in a variable, or passed around as data. It avoids mutable states and unwanted, unexpected, and undetected side effects, including malware and ransomware. The PP250 exploited these facts to purge errors and prevent interference using symbolic capability-limited addressing.

The λ-calculus is simple, powerful, elegant, and scientifically comprehensive. The symbols simplify reasoning about computation and logic. It has many advantages in computer science, mathematics, philosophy, linguistics, cryptography, and artificial intelligence. For example, additional power exists because symbols are first-class values the language can manipulate as objects, and an object can be any abstract digital item, not just an algorithm, but also a constant, a class, or another complex application. PP250's machine code programs demonstrate this power that exists without undetected malware or concerns about unwanted interference and unspecified side effects. See Equation 1, Symbolic machine code Using Capability-Limited-Object-Oriented-Statement for Telecoms.

Functional programming languages, including Capability-Limited-Object-Oriented- Machine-Code, use symbolic names to assign variables, pass arguments, return results from functions, or compose high-order symbols. It allows functions to receive complex arguments or return them as results. Higher-order functions enable potent abstractions and expressive programs that, when secured as machine code, create industrial-strength computer science across cyberspace without the flaws of centralization, fragmentation, and side effects like malware or crimes that all lead to digital dictatorship.

For example, a telecommunications namespace could write the following expression in a single fail-safe computer command that returns a private but potentially global 'digital twin'[14] of a telephone call[15].

$$myConnection = CALL(Switch.Connect(me, myMother))$$

Equation 1, Symbolic machine code Using Capability-Limited-Object-Oriented-Statement for Telecoms

---

14   A digital twin is a virtual representation — a true-to-reality simulation of physics, and materials — of a real- world physical asset or system, which is continuously updated. Source NAVIDA

15   See Book 1: Civilizing Cyberspace pp 96

The power of such an individual and personal command overwhelms all aspects of binary computer power. It demonstrates the individual privacy and the functional power of Capability-Limited-Object-Oriented-Machine-Code as a Church-Turing machine without decades of centralized and offline baggage distracting binary computer programs from the task at hand.

Binary machine code is limited to passing insecure values. They are easily forged, misinterpreted, and misunderstood. These numeric, binary variables have constrained and slowed software progress since World War II. The symbolic, object-oriented statement above uses names to represent complex ideas as identified programmed abstract objects. In this case, a phone call or a telecommunication switching system could also improve by directly adding any named AI service as a symbolic statement in machine code without any binary baggage caused by centralization and dictatorial branded operating systems. Such interactions are always secure and prevent AI-breakout.

Binary computers can only represent two simple values, either 0 or 1. Nowhere close to representing a digital twin of any abstract kind. Thus, the resulting machine code is bulky, clumsy, opaque, divorced from security, and hard to understand. On the other hand, symbolic computing is natural, readable, secure, robust, and streamlined to the maximum at no additional cost. Equally important, symbolic computing is modular, with functional digital boundaries that can be defended and protected as an immutable digital fortress in a hostile battlefield that distinguishes information types as private sets in each digital twin.

These sets are securely isolated under each programmer's audited control. Further, the immutable names never change and can be protected as secret capability tokens, which can also act as passwords and identity permissions. These namespaces can today be protected by blockchain abstractions. So, while binary computing is vulnerable to attacks using malware to corrupt the physical addresses or data values, symbolic computing is modular and can be secured in a Church-Turing Machine using the boundary protection of digital ironwork called capability-limited addressing.

Furthermore, the enhanced powers of cryptography, AI, blockchains, and other complex functions can be directly used in secure machine code statements today, further enhancing Church-Turing Machines' power.

Even when a programming language supports functional programming, the compiled code is trapped in one compiled and isolated binary image. The compiler cannot support networked function abstractions smoothly because this requires operating system changes. Compare the PP250 using immutable tokens as the abstract names in capability-limited object-oriented machine code. Now, abstract concepts have the potential to span the globe figuratively and metaphorically. Also, as shown above, the tokens make the machine code readable and understandable.

Ada Lovelace programmed mathematics expressions that work similarly but were limited to Charles Babbage's physical mechanics, the Analytical Engine. Nevertheless, Ada's vision recognized the capability of abstractions when she envisioned that computers could compose music, create art, and write literature. She did all this before tragically dying at the young age of thirty-six in 1852.

Compiled programming languages are confined to one compilation at a time, operating in an isolated single machine that can only interconnect through the centralized operating system. This communication baggage is exposed, opaque, and unfair, and it is subject to attack by hidden highway malware and spying by digital dictators. PP250's use of abstract nomenclature, akin to Theoretical Mathematics, connects globally in literal and figurative senses. Its abstract machine code transcends the physical world and boundary limitations, adding power and security across networked cyberspace.

Lovelace anticipated this with astonishing foresight; she predicted what Steve Jobs achieved with Objective-C and the Apple Mac in 1984, the applications of object-oriented software to music composition, art creation, and literary writing. She did all this in the 1840s, before her premature death, and a century and a half before Steve Jobs proved her right.

Machine code is the most powerful of all programming languages. It even allows enemies to take control of computer science through malware. Thus, machine code is perfected when implemented as a secure, functional programming language reinforced by capability-limited addressing. When the power of clean object-oriented languages like Smalltalk and Objective-C, rather than C++ [16] , are used to create Capability Limited Object-Oriented Machine Code, proven programmable security benefits and fail-safe computations are realized. Innovation creates a safe, efficient, intelligent system of globally secure networked namespace structures for nations, businesses, and individuals, all functionally protected within digital cyberspace. Digitally virtualizing the foundation principles of theoretical mathematics makes computers simple to understand, with affordable high performance and the engineered reliability to win WW III.

Following the λ-calculus and the Church-Turing Thesis is scientifically superior to unreliable functionally limited binary computers using only numbers and shared physical addresses for computation on the surface of computer science where all problems originate. The central operating systems need access to privileged hardware, allowing a secret surveillance system to inspect every communication except those that matter most when malware strikes. They are irredeemably vulnerable to hacking, malware, corruption, and cyber conflict. In contrast, symbolic computers are fail-safe, comprehensible computational machines using readable, flawlessly secure machine code to exchange complex functional operations—a trusted machine built from secure digital ironwork, the golden tokens of symbolic computation, and Capability Limited addressing.

Symbolic computing aligns with theoretical mathematics and the pure science of abstract mental concepts. It enables a networked cyberspace for individuals and democratic nations as a reliable, scalable, evolvable platform to solve complex problems in any abstract or distributed field without the overheads and disruptions from centralized baggage. The Capability-Limited-Object-Oriented-

---

16   C++ has a weak object-orientation that creates many unforced errors, from fundamental syntax, and basic data structures errors for beginners, to advanced concepts like object-oriented programming (OOP), and efficient memory management for experienced developers. Source Codesignal

Machine-Code is enhanced when integrated with complex fields, including blockchains, artificial intelligence, cryptography, financial modelling, game theory, and more, unlocking new possibilities of integrated software applications to improve life without any baggage or downsides.

The conclusion is clear: the government should fund working examples of Church-Turing Machines that protect the USA by following science and issuing it freely, as was done with the COVID-19 vaccination. It enables competition and the natural advantages of the λ- calculus to win and save the scientific foundation of the future. These inherent advantages guarantee success in solving the future problems of a rapidly evolving cyber society. The computer industry can then embrace symbolic computing as the basement technology of computer hardware for networked function abstraction. The result is a robust, potent, digitally secure global platform that is an inherently scientific, reliable, secure, individually private, future-safe solution democratically structured to meet the international needs of civilized progress.

THEORETICAL MATHEMATICS

Theoretical Mathematics is distinct from the physical world, which consists of tangible objects with measurable properties like size, mass, colour, and reliability. Theoretical Mathematics is a pure science of abstract concepts. Ideas that exist only in the mind, without physical attributes. Like mathematical objects, the only criterion for judging ideas is their reliable correctness. Capability-Limited-Object-Oriented-Machine-Code directly addresses the relationship between named ideas, programmed functions, and reliability in a coherent digital namespace. The most basic namespace is the mathematics namespace, first engineered by Charles Babbage for his unfinished Analytical Engine.

As a discipline, computer science involves translating the complex cognitive processes of Theoretical Mathematics into concrete, reproducible, flawlessly programmed, fail-safe phenomena for scientific research or practical human applications. The key to this translation begins with scientific symbols representing mathematics as a functional process—a scientific cognitive construct of explicitly defined tasks matching the exact meaning of unique, immutable symbols.

Table 5 Example Symbols Used in Theoretical Mathematics by Subject	
Arithmetic	Addition (+), and Subtraction (-), Multiplication (x), Division (/)
Algebra	Equals (=), Not equal (≠), Greater than (>), Less than (<), Greater than orequal to (≥), Less than or equal to (≤), Plus-minus (±), Minus-plus (∓), Infinity (∞)
Set Theory	Element of (∈), Not an element of (∉), Subset (⊂), Superset (⊃), Union (∪), Intersection (∩), Empty set (∅), Universal set (U)
Logic	And (∧), Or (∨), Not (¬), Implies (⇒), If, and only if (⇔), For all (∀), There exists (∃)
Calculus	Derivative (d/dx), Partial derivative (∂/∂x), Integral (∫), Double integral (∫∫), Triple integral: (∫∫∫), Limit (lim), Summation (∑), Product (∏)
Geometry	Angle (∠), Triangle (△), Parallel to (∥), Perpendicular to (⊥), Similar To (~), Congruent to (≅)
Statistics	Probability (P), Expected value (E), Variance (Var), Standard deviation (σ), Normal distribution (N(μ,σ))

Consider the immutable symbols used above for teaching and applying mathematics worldwide as a programming language computed by humans. Table 5 Example Symbols Used in Theoretical Mathematics by Subject above shows this machine code of the mind that began like human languages at the birth of civilization and with a corresponding machine called the abacus. They name the function abstraction of numbers as the foundation objects of Theoretical Mathematics.

Symbolic computation is as central to computer science as to Theoretical Mathematics. Understanding and processing symbols as scientific functions in calculations is vital to both fields, and the connection is made evident by the Church Turing Thesis. The thesis is founded on Alonzo Church's λ-calculus that encapsulates Alan's Turing Machine as atomic computations that hide and protect the implementation details from observation, interference, and attack, leaving only intrinsic functionality to resolve. The λ-calculus establishes the link between computing as a real-world process and a mental exercise.

In contrast, binary computers are primitive. They operate physically using memory locations, peripheral connections, and network ports. There are no guard rails or beads to keep things on track. Rather than symbolic logic, they rely on programming languages, compilers, and operating systems to indirectly provide the symbolic aspects of computer science that binary computers inherently lack. The need for translation always remains, but when fragmented, it is messy because it operates, and subtle conflicts between several levels exist, all well removed from the machine code. Furthermore, the imperfect results are trapped in a single binary computer networked by other branded symbolic disruption levels. The physical machine instructions are quickly and easily composed incorrectly or reassembled out of sequence by the program and instantly turn from Jekyll to Hyde[17].

Thus, the binary computer is unsafe because it cannot represent abstract ideas cleanly. The binary twins of an idea are always fragmented, preventing easy sharing. Variables are limited to numbers. On the other hand, the human mind and a Church-Turing Machine are designed to share complex ideas cleanly by using a symbolic name to represent individual ideas. These ideas exist in cyberspace as a λ-calculus function abstraction, a digital twin of the idea. Ideas and objects of any complexity are represented as abstractions, a complex dream for Ada Lovelace or when designed for a digital computer, a λ-calculus Namespace, a function abstraction, a block of Capability-Limited-Object-Oriented-Machine-Code or a specially formatted digital object.

Moreover, every machine instruction is engineered to be fail-safe, preventing malware and catching errors. Programming mistakes, loading errors, time-sharing hazards, outside interference, and malware are the perils in binary programs that immediately and irreparably damage results. A Church-Turing Machine detects every error as data-tight, function-tight digital objects. One is just a crude programmer's workshop built by the first generation of beginners. On the other hand, industrial-strength computer science applies engineering to software to sustain a democratic digital society in the open-ended future.

---

17   Jekyll, and Hyde refer to something with different sides in nature, from R.L. Stevenson 1886 Gothic novella

Imperative commands, the RISC instructions, are unassembled nuts and bolts put together on the fly without any rules. Mistakes are easy to make, and some simple errors are catastrophic. When Turing made the first proposal, the algorithm was an atomic computation directly compatible with the λ-calculus. These named algorithms were stored coherently on individual paper tapes, fully compatible with symbolic addressing as used by Alonzo's masterpiece, the λ-calculus.

Ten years later, in 1945, after WW II, when von Neumann ignored the λ-calculus and the Church-Turing Thesis, he lost symbolic addressing and turned to physical addressing. Secure algorithmic independence was surrendered, and he dangerously shared the full- sized physical address to the total memory unit of the binary computer without any guard rails to prevent interference. This scientific mistake is the root cause of every technical problem in binary cyberspace. Binary computers are, in truth, not computer science.

Since then, the computer industry has unsuccessfully struggled, at a vast cost, to limit this mistake that fragments through unseen side effects to ricochet within shared memory and out onto the network. Programmers do not directly control either the side effects or outside interference. These errors, including hacks and malware, randomly generate unacceptable conditions by surprise from another fragmented place and time. An individual program's integrity cannot be guaranteed in shared binary memory, and errors cannot be recognized when and where they occur.

At very high-performance overheads, the central operating systems and compiled code try to prevent hackers, crooks, spies, and enemies from breaking in, but too often, they fail. Malware can break into the cockpit and take over control. A Confused Deputy attack is used by ransomware if stolen credentials do not work. These worst-case attacks overturn the centralized single point of failure to destroy the operating system's security and reliability, spreading the attack over the network and freezing everything.

It is unavoidable that cyberspace is a shared platform for the everlasting future of every citizen in every nation worldwide. Any flaw can compromise the integrity of critical functionality across all international boundaries. It is the recipe for the polarizing conflicts between uncooperative citizens and conflicted nations. Flaws in cyberspace allow malicious actors to exploit vulnerabilities, steal data, disrupt services, sabotage systems, and cause harm to users and democratic society. Centralization increases digital dictatorship as good intentions turn to ruthless attempts to prevent tragic attacks. The flaws in cyberspace undermine trust, confidence, and innovation. Following science and mathematics laws, computers must be designed and maintained to the highest quality, reliability, and strength standards. Nothing less removes the existential risks to the future of civilization.

Cyberspace as an international platform must be free from errors, bugs, glitches, hacks, malware, ransomware, and other threats, particularly every single point of failure that jeopardises the integrity and stability of international society. Cyberspace must be a platform that automatically supports progress and prosperity. It cannot be a continual source of risk and uncertainty, the everlasting battlefield for WW III, and the lurking threats of another accidental but more serious Big Freeze. Digital complexity makes these mistakes inevitable, increasing in scale and making it difficult to recover quickly. Therefore, computers must be proven as scientific machines that can be trusted internationally. Then, the flawless and fail-safe details include full-time guard rails like the abacus, guaranteeing the international civilization of society.

Binary computers cannot do this. They are not self-regulated machines. They are a collection of imperative commands built for mainframes that were never expected to be networked. It is impossible to sustain them adequately in a dynamic network of interconnected enemies, crooks, spies, and evolving global threats. Only the science of λ- calculus bridges this gap safely by attaching logic to physics, using symbolic names to match physical hardware with the logic of programmed digital objects. The success of binary computers is a testament to the limits of computing. However, since binary computers cannot survive the threats of hacking and malware today, they certainly cannot survive future attacks created by artificial intelligence, trained to write malware by a determined enemy of the state or gangs of crooks.

Architecture	Characteristics	Result
Binary Computers Share Hardware Centralized Failures	Unregulated single-points-of- failure created by mainframes, not used in networks. It cannot withstand hacking and malware threats, the endless WW III or a future attack synchronized globally by artificial intelligence.	Statically bound offline and physically addressed. It cannot sustain functionality in a dynamic network of interconnected enemies and evolving global threats.
Church-Turing Machine Distributed Software Type Secure Boundaries	The science of λ-calculus bridges the safety gap by binding logic to physics, using symbolic names to match physical hardware with the logic of programmed digital objects.	Performance improvements, future-safe, scientifically bound by the λ-calculus as a network-ready, capability- secure digital machine.

Table 6 Comparing Computer Architectures

Global cyberspace dominates our future, and software has unprecedented power in society. It must remain perfectly safe for anyone to learn, use, abuse, and misuse, not just experts but all. Machine code is the Lingua Franca of cyber society and the future of civilization. It must work for all, including the unskilled and the untrained. It is necessary for humanity's collective survival and progress. The invisible power for good and evil now encircles the world and brings undetected harm to everyday life from foreign sources. Intentional crimes and undetected foreign corruption have reached a point that can only be fixed by the Federal Government. After all, only the Federal Government is responsible for international affairs.

Too many are involved in the messy interworking connections of binary cyberspace. Skilled staff is in short supply and getting scarcer, while the patches are more challenging to apply. The risks increase. Anyone can learn to use a smartphone or a laptop to launch an attack from the far side of the world and cause severe, lasting damage, not just in cyberspace but in any service industry, from water to airlines or police and emergency to the armed forces.

Lacking science, the many brands and models of computers are all different, too many to understand, each influenced by corporate interests of the day that appealed to various customers. These branded machines all run without scientific or mathematical guard rails. Instead, everything is designed offline, demanding strange conventions called best practices. The binary computer is only sophisticated in terms of virtual memory.

Unlike industrial machines designed to protect the operators, binary computers can run wild, as tragically demonstrated by the 737 MAX calamities. The crashes in Indonesia and Ethiopia killed 346 passengers and crew members when the software repeatedly pushed the plane's nose down, overriding the pilots' attempts to correct this.

These terrible catastrophes were human design errors not unlike the CrowdStrike Big Freeze. But malware can do the same. It can also hide inside good programs that cannot be locked out of a binary cockpit. Instead, they invade and take over computations like terrorists with intolerable, unexpected results. Binary computers have no doors to lock or keys to protect functionality. Just one incorrect line of unregulated binary machine code can change everything. Privacy cannot exist because everything is blindly trusted to work as expected in a civilized society. Uncivilized global cyberspace has changed the rules, and computer science must improve.

Hackers, crooks, spies, and enemies operate online but are out of reach of national law and order. They disrupt computer science by pursuing malicious objectives. Increasingly, software controls our lives. Always remember how the pilots of the Boeing 737 MAX were locked out by software that caused two crashes, killing all on board. Binary computers let us down, mislead, and kill us. They lack the industrial strength needed for nations to survive, prosper, and remain productive, skilled, and democratic.

Individuals are in the hands of unknown design teams who shape the software but cannot control security. Ransomware can halt a hospital, a city, or a business overnight. An app can hide malware or a bug. Foreign enemies can undermine national security and hide malware for a planned later attack. In specific ways, artificial intelligence already exceeds human ability. Soon, AI may break out to create superhuman malware for our enemies. Then, humanity is just a curiosity for a zoo, condemned by the invisible, opaque power of unscientific human folly.

Binary cyberspace lacks the strength needed for the endless future. As the invisible power of software spreads, it changes traditional, stable operations, values, families, and nations. Unintended side effects permeate life, and trying to stop them with patching increases the authoritarian power of the digital dictators who created the problem. Government and suppliers collude, and the unwanted side effect is the Orwellian dictatorship already well- advanced in China, Russia, North Korea, and Iran.

The root cause of these problems is a lack of computational science in binary computers. Ignoring the laws of λ-calculus established by the Church-Turing Thesis was a severe mistake that cannot continue. Various brands of proprietary binary computers emerged; they all ignore these laws rooted in Theoretical Mathematics as the foundation of computer science. It is time for the Federal Government to act responsibly and defend international cyberspace by developing a new generation of digital computers to solve all the dilemmas created since WW II. The science exists; international computational security is a matter of national survival, and to do nothing is simply unacceptable, irresponsible government ignorance or neglect.

THE BIG FREEZE

Binary computers still follow the first generation of digitally shared hardware proposed by von Neumann after World War II in 1946, a decade after the teamwork of Church and Turing decoded computer science through the λ-calculus. Nevertheless, binary computers prospered as a standalone solution without the λ-calculus. Locked-in rooms without network connections, the mainframe age led by IBM snowballed using offline compilers and imperative commands as procedural programming languages.

Early programming languages like COBOL were designed to build centralized, shared binary images by offline compilers in a statically linked imperative procedural paradigm. Hardware centralization, operating systems, and business needs of the mainframe did not follow the theoretical foundations of computer science from Church and Turing. Instead, they centralized complexity into increasingly intricate procedures and patched any flaws. The result was spaghetti code prone to bugs, complications, and security vulnerabilities that could not be easily debugged or patched. Furthermore, the process created vendor lock-in and backward compatibility issues that hampered innovation and interoperability. It remains a recurring problem for every generation of beginners trying to understand the various brands of binary computer nonsense. The difficulty of understanding binary computers causes low staff certification rates and staff shortages, and no one is adequately trained to resolve the problem of single-point-of-failure and a Big Freeze.

In the 1960s, minicomputers evolved, all different in detail. Still, everyone followed IBM's lead, using centralized, page-based memory hardware and a privileged operating system supervisor like Multics that MIT sanctified for the Cold War era. After decades, the centralized single point of failure led to cybercrime, ransomware, and the first network-wide Big Freeze experience on July 19th, 2024. It was a calculated risk for binary computers created by von Neumann's cut-off, but it is an unacceptable failure in global cyberspace.

On the other hand, as a public utility, the telecommunication industry applies standards that reflect society's need to prevent any widespread outage. The UK standard of a five- decade MTBF forced the PP250 to solve problems the computer industry could ignore. Thus, the PP250 researched the Church-Turing Thesis and restored the science of the λ-calculus from 1936 to create a democratic distributed solution for software to achieve Industrial- Strength Computer Science.

Cyberspace deserves the status of a Public Utility to prevent service outages like the Big Freeze. The highest reliability standards should apply to cyberspace and drive the computer industry to improve. Cyberspace already acts as a public utility, but nothing is done unless a public commission exists to apply the standards PP250 had to meet.

Centralization continues, binary compilations are complicated, and software development slows, so suppliers enforce backwards-compatible machine code to limit new software development efforts and run earlier software without recompilation. As a result, the binary installation's size and complexity became impossibly slow to retest exhaustively. At first, teams of IT experts, as well as corporate masters, worked behind closed doors, using shift work and reruns to hide unfound bugs from the results. However, when personal computing began, personal computers escaped the locked rooms of Information Technology departments. Crude networks began, and then another critical change evolved: hacking. However, the computer industry makes no serious attempt to stop hackers by design or remove centralization and the single points of failure.

As a public utility, hacking would be a crime. However, in computer science, hackers are admired for their technical skills and creativity. Some hackers have used their abilities to improve flawed binary software, find vulnerabilities, create new software solutions, and promote the oxymoron of ethical hacking. The programming community praises them. Some created star open-source products:

1. Kevin Mitnick was a hacker in the 1990s who broke into the private networks of companies, universities, and government agencies, often using social engineering techniques to trick people into revealing their credentials. He was arrested in 1995, serving five years in prison, forbidden to use any electronic device. After his release, he became a security consultant and author, helping organizations protect themselves from hacking. He founded Mitnick Security Consulting to offer penetration testing and security training.

2. Linux is now one of the most popular and influential open-source software projects, with millions of contributors and users. As a student at the University of Helsinki, Linus Torvalds started Linux as a hobby in 1991 after he hacked the operating system Minix code, making it available for anyone to modify and redistribute. Linux now powers servers, supercomputers, smartphones, and embedded devices. Thousands of volunteers and companies support it and contribute code, documentation, testing, and support. The license is under the GNU General Public License (GPL), allowing anyone to use, modify, and distribute it if they follow these terms.

3. Browsers were invented by Tim Berners-Lee, who started the World Wide Web to allow access to and the sharing of documents as a software engineer at CERN, the European Organization for Nuclear Research. He linked documents using hypertext and downloaded them over a network. He wrote the first web browser and server in 1990 and

launched the first website in 1991[18]. He defined protocols for HTML, HTTP, and URL, which are used today. He set up the World Wide Web Consortium and advocates for openness, neutrality, and privacy on the web.

4. Apache is web server software that handles browsers' requests and delivers web pages, images, and other content. It is the most widely used web server, powering over 40% of all websites. Apache is developed by the Apache Software Foundation, a non-profit organization that oversees hundreds of open-source projects. It is licensed under the Apache License, which grants users the right to use, copy, modify, and distribute it with minimal restrictions[19].

5. Mozilla is behind the Firefox web browser, the Thunderbird email client, and other software products, dedicated to a free and open web that respects user privacy, security, and choice. It is governed by the Mozilla Foundation, a non-profit organization that supports open-source development, education, and advocacy, and is licensed under various open-source licenses, such as the Mozilla Public License (MPL), the GNU GPL, and the GNU Lesser General Public License (LGPL).

6. WordPress software powers over 40% of all websites, including blogs, news, and e-commerce sites; it is a content management system (CMS) that allows easy creation and management of an online presence. WordPress is developed by a community of developers, designers, writers, and users who contribute themes, plugins, translations, and support. It is licensed under the GNU GPL, which includes the freedom to use, modify, and share it.

7. Python is a programming language. It is used for web development, data analysis, machine learning, scripting, and more. It is known for simplicity, readability, and versatility and was developed by the Python Software Foundation, a non-profit organization to manage the language. It is licensed under the Python Software License and compatible with the

---

18   Tim Berners-Lee | MIT CSAIL
19   What is Apache? - King Host Coupon

GNU GPL, allowing users to use, modify, and distribute it without restrictions. A feature of Python is support for multiple paradigms, including functional programming consistent with Capability- Limited-Object-Oriented-Machine-Code, treating computations to evaluate mathematical functions. As with λ-calculus, it avoids changing state and mutable data like binary code. It is the best candidate language as the IDE assembler for the Dream Machine.

This evident enthusiasm for open-source software needs to be directed at the next- generation solution for cyberspace. Creating a secure Church-Turing Machine using Capability-Limited-Object-Oriented-Machine-Code is the first step as a Federal Government project and initially as a free distribution. Competition through the ideals of the global open-source community and the advanced programming capabilities of the λ- calculus technology is a game changer. The democratization of computer science decreases staff shortages and increases productivity dramatically through quality, numbers, interest level, potency, and staff engagement.

The first step forward in next-generation programming is avoiding binary side effects that allow hackers and malware to misuse the unintended side effects or manipulate external states. Using higher-order functions, which take functions as arguments and return them as results, Python's functional programming can directly use the power of Capability-Limited- Object-Oriented-Machine-Code to write concise, clear, and modular code that is easily tested and debugged with the built-in error checking of a Church-Turing computer like the PP250, and the proposed Dream Machine.

If not, hacking, malware, ransomware, and the Big Freeze undermine all these notable success stories. Hacking began as a prank by computer enthusiasts who explored the limits of binary technology by challenging the security of systems. Early hackers coined the term "hacking" to describe their activities, which they considered creative and playful. However, hacking has become a criminal activity, as some use their skills to steal data, money, or identities and damage or disrupt systems.

It came to the fore by 1988 when the Morris worm infected thousands of computers connected to the ARPANET, the Internet's precursor. He intended to measure the size of the network, but due to a code error, it excessively replicated itself and slowed down the infected machines. Morris was the first person convicted under the Computer Fraud and Abuse Act[20].

Sony Pictures was hacked in 2014 by the Guardians of Peace, affiliated with North Korea. They breached the private network of Sony Pictures Entertainment and leaked confidential data, including personal information about employees and celebrities, as well as unreleased films, scripts, and emails. They threatened to launch attacks on cinemas that showed the film The Interview, a comedy about a plot to assassinate the North Korean leader, Kim Jong-un. The US government blamed North Korea for the attack, but the regime denied any involvement. No one was punished beyond Sony staff.

The WannaCry ransomware attack occurred in 2017 and affected over 200,000 computers in 150 countries[21]. The attack exploited a vulnerability in the Windows operating system that was leaked by hackers known as The Shadow Brokers, who claimed to have stolen it from the National Security Agency (NSA). The attack encrypted the data on the infected machines and demanded a ransom in Bitcoin to unlock them. They disrupted many organizations, including hospitals, banks, and government agencies. A British security researcher stopped the attack by registering a domain name as a kill switch for the ransomware.

Hacking would never occur if digital computers were engineered to survive as Industrial- Strength Computers designed to meet the non-stop standards of Public Utilities. The PP250 was designed for the phone service that required computer control systems with a 50-year MTBF for the combined hardware and software as a system, and the requirement was met. Industry standards like MTBF would

---

20   My First Call to a Convicted Hacker - | MSSP Alert

21   Cybersecurity for Business Resilience | Business Experts Gulf (bemea. com)

force the computer industry to replace the privileged operating system, the superuser, and all Administrator single-point-of-failure. Improvements would occur because they are the root cause of ransomware and Blue Screen outages.

Instead, at prohibitive cost and poor results, a massive industrial effort by corporate IT departments and network surveillance by secret government agencies reduce but do not remove these outages. So, backward compatibility and single points of failure remain, and improvements stagnate, preventing individuals who lack the time and the training required to spend preventing malware attacks. The centralized overheads continue to grow, and nothing is done to solve the problem. Attacks from criminal gangs worldwide and enemy states forever flood binary cyberspace and work to deliver the Big Freeze.

One of the consequences of the binary computer's unreliability and insecurity is the high turnover rate of chief information officers (CIOs), who oversee an organisation's IT infrastructure and strategy. According to a 2020 study by Korn Ferry, the average tenure of a CIO in the US was 4.1 years, compared to 5.1 years for CEOs. The study reports that voluntary CIO departures at 38% are the highest among all C-suite positions, confirming they face significant challenges and job pressures, managing complex legacy systems, coping with cyber threats, aligning IT with business goals, and keeping up with technological innovations. Job satisfaction and performance are low, as are the support and understanding of colleagues who expect results and do not grasp the 7x24 urgency and complexity that IT departments face. Consequently, IT staff turnover and early retirement are high, increasing leadership gaps, staff shortages, and continuity problems. The democratization of computer science is the only way to resolve this problem.

According to a 2021 report by CompTIA, global IT skills are estimated at 40%, so four out of ten positions are unfilled, all due to the lack of qualified talent and branded skills. The report identified demand in the top 10 IT skills as cybersecurity, cloud computing, data analytics, network engineering, software development, project management, digital transformation, IT support, artificial intelligence, and the Internet of Things.

Thus, keeping up requires constant learning and endless recruiting time as technology evolves rapidly and new threats emerge frequently. The administrators are running in place and lack the time, resources, or motivation to keep up with trends and learn the latest round of incomprehensible best practices. It means rapid skill obsolescence, inferior performance, more outages, and additional shortages. It is a downward spiral.

Moreover, the education system cannot produce enough IT graduates with the necessary skills and certifications to meet the constantly growing industry demand. Only 25% of IT workers have formal qualifications, half the number in a non-IT field, and 26% have no degree, indicating a mismatch between academic curriculums and employer expectations.

The skill shortage indicates the peculiar nature of Information Technology and the urgent need for democratization. It severely impacts the quality and security of binary computers and personal computing. Organizations cannot evolve, manage, and protect their IT systems and data effectively, exposing them to cyberattacks, downtime, errors, and inefficiency. Furthermore, without skilled, competent CIOs, organizations cannot refine their IT strategy to meet business goals, innovate, compete in the digital economy, and leverage the opportunities and benefits of emerging technologies. The skill shortage in the IT sector is a significant obstacle to digital transformation and the resilience of organizations and society, and it is a critical factor behind the looming threat of another Big Freeze.

Delta Air Lines CEO Ed Bastian reported a $500 million loss due to CrowdStrike's Big Freeze affecting operations, leading to over 5,000 flight cancellations and delays in recovery. The

U.S. Department of Transportation is investigating Delta's situation management and customer communication. At the same time, Delta got attorney David Boies on board and alerted CrowdStrike and

Microsoft of impending legal action. "We have no choice," Bastian commented on CNBC, citing significant revenue loss and daily costs for compensations and accommodations while attempting to support their customers during this period.

It is not computer science. It is branded chaos. No one can keep up, no patches or virus scanners can fix a single point of failure, individuals cross their fingers, the government obfuscates, and the administration of computer networks as a single point of failure is in deep trouble. Binary cyberspace is too opaque and unnecessarily complex after decades of centralized misdirection. Without the immutable digital gold of the Church-Turing Thesis, the binary details are unfathomable, unreadable brands of gobbledygook correctly decoded by no one, even the original author, if they could be found.

Binary computers are scary, skills are scarce, and branded best practices are strange, unscientific, unreasonable, and ever-changing. Even experts only understand one brand's best practices. Finding and fixing problems gets increasingly slow and complex and worsens as time passes. The unscientific foundation of the binary computer is a self-perpetuating torment, a digital roadblock to the improvement of cyber society. Widespread confusion, digital chaos, and a lack of skills are losing WW III.

The situation is more cataclysmic than the global shutdown caused by COVID-19. Cyber society cannot prosper or even progress when branded binary cyberspace is so confusing and, at the same time, increasingly dangerous to the progress of democracy. The foretaste on July 19th, 2024, was not an attack. Instead, the superuser administrators became the enemy, and CrowdStrike distributed a flawed software update. The problem is not fixed. It is the hardware nature of privileged centralization in binary computers. The incident caused massive damage to the reputation of CrowdStrike and hurt their customers. Airports were jam-packed with passengers who could not fly for days, and a week later, they were still jam- packed with luggage.

Table 7 Airport Congestion Chaos Caused by a Big Freeze

Dramatically, for the first time, it exposed the fragility of binary-based cybersecurity and the significance of single points of failure. There is no definitive answer to how many Windows systems experienced a Blue Screen. One source, the Microsoft Security Response Center (MSRC), reported that the vulnerability affected 84,000 Windows systems globally, causing 32% of them to experience a blue screen. Another source is the Cybersecurity and Infrastructure Security Agency (CISA), which estimated that the Blue Screen of Death froze 12,000 US Windows computers on July 19th, 2024, Big Freeze.

Embarrassment and secrecy mean the actual number may never be known. More than 100,000, depending on how many countries and regions report in full. This alarming number indicates the risks, severity, and impact of single-point-of-failure in cyberspace on global society. The impact grows with time and emphasises the need for hardware and software upgrades to achieve a robust, secure cyber platform that eliminates vulnerability, protects society from malicious code, removes single points of failure, and democratises the required skill set.

Industrial-Strength Computer Science does all this and never allows such an outage. Backwards, binary computers were frozen to reduce costs and increase mainframe profits. Still, enemies with AI can now initiate targeted superhuman attacks that amplify the shortage of skilled staff and bring progress to a halt. The industry difficulties grow indefinitely.

More ingenious attackers and stupid administrators have a sophistication that confounds the skilled staff, who remain forever in short supply. It stagnates the industry as incomprehensible binary details grow in depth and detail. National, industrial, and individual cyber catastrophes can strike simultaneously in many directions and places.

It is sad and unnecessary since second-generation symbolic computers solve every unscientific binary problem by following the example of Babbage, Lovelace, Church's λ- calculus, and the PP250: Data-tight and function-tight abstractions free cyberspace of undetected crime. The natural science of λ-calculus was defined by Alonzo Church while guiding his Doctoral student Alan Turing to invent the atomic binary computer. Their combined thesis unites both sides of computational complexity as the simplified scientific bridge between logic and physics.

The bridge between logic and physics hides every implementation detail behind individual λ-calculus symbols as dynamically bound function abstractions. In this architecture, the engine is atomic computing, just one private function abstraction at a time, exactly as Turing first proposed and precisely as needed by the individual symbols of theoretical science. These computations work like a schoolroom of children following the instruction programmed abstractly from a namespace written by a teacher on a schoolroom chalkboard and then computed in parallel as individual threads calculated by each child working independently in private.

The symbolic names used by the teacher ground each child's computational thread in the branch of science taught by the teacher, where the students substitute their specific private variables to solve their unique problem. Namespace boundaries distinguish between physics, mathematics, chemistry, logic, or, as Ada recognized, philosophy, art, music, literature, and anything else in nature in the human mind. Ada Lovelace had her vision two centuries ago, long before the Church-Turing Thesis and digital computers, before she was thirty in the 1840s. To ignore this profound, successful history of private computational threads dating back to the birth of civilization is collective, national suicide driven by industrial greed and the stupidity of the followers of John von Neumann's ego.

Everyone has lost valuable data held by binary computers, but it never needs to happen when computer software is engineered and digital security is program-controlled. Undetected errors are the root cause of all forms of malware. It exists because binary computers work physically instead of logically, using dangerously shared address space instead of the private symbols used in a human mind. Worse still, binary computers are centralized, so malware focuses on this single point of failure to overturn logic, take control, encrypt, and freeze everything physical.

Cities, hospitals, schools, the police and emergency services, local and national governments, and the armed forces are all susceptible targets for the ultimate single point of failure as a Big Freeze. Our enemies are working hard, implanting booby traps and opening channels in advance to guarantee that the instantaneous attack freezes the nation all at once. The scope of a coordinated Big Freeze exceeds the damage done by prior ransomware attacks worldwide, pandemics on the scale of COVID-19.

1. In May 2017, the WannaCry ransomware infected more than 200,000 computers in

2. 150 countries, targeting hospitals, banks, government agencies, and other organizations. The attackers demanded $300 to $600 in Bitcoin to unlock the encrypted files. The attack was stopped by an administrator who found a kill switch hidden in the malware, but not before it caused an estimated $4 billion in damages.

3. In June 2017, the NotPetya ransomware spread through a compromised update of Ukrainian accounting software, affecting thousands of computers in Ukraine, Russia, Poland, Germany, France, and other countries. The malware

encrypted the master boot record of the infected machines, making them unusable, and demanded $300 in Bitcoin for the decryption key. However, the attackers did not provide a working recovery mechanism, making the attack more of a destructive cyberattack than ransomware. The attack caused an estimated $10 billion in damages, affecting major companies like Maersk, Merck, FedEx, and Mondelez.

4. In March 2018, the SamSam ransomware targeted the city of Atlanta, Georgia, disrupting many municipal services and operations. The attackers demanded

5. $51,000 in Bitcoin to restore access to the encrypted files, but the city refused to pay. The attack cost the city more than $17 million in recovery expenses and lost revenues.

6. In May 2021, the Colonial Pipeline, which supplies about 45% of the fuel consumed on the East Coast of the United States, was hit by a ransomware attack attributed to a cybercriminal group called Dark Side. The attack forced the company to shut down its pipeline operations for several days, causing widespread fuel shortages and price spikes in many states. The company paid the attackers $4.4 million in Bitcoin to restore access but later recovered funds with the help of the FBI.

7. In July 2021, the Kaseya ransomware attack affected over 1,000 businesses and organizations worldwide, including schools, hospitals, supermarkets, and travel agencies. The attack exploited a vulnerability in the software of Kaseya, a company that provides IT management services to small and medium-sized businesses. The attackers, believed to be part of the *REvil* group, demanded $70 million in Bitcoin for a universal decryption tool. The attack was described as one of the largest and most sophisticated ransomware attacks in history.

8. People woke on July 19th, 2024, to technological chaos as Microsoft suffered a massive global IT outage, impacting airports, stocks, airlines, banks, and broadcasters worldwide.

Most importantly, the US emergency 911 call centres were hit, as was the London Stock Exchange. It was linked to a faulty update from CrowdStrike concerning Windows PCs and services worldwide.

Despite the discombobulating social impact, the costs, and the damage, these Big Freezes are here to stay for as long as binary computers exist. The digital dictators make too much money, first selling the problem and then selling snake oil potions to the citizen pioneers. The digital dictators are unwilling to risk an alternative to binary computers. Thus, undetected corruption and crimes continue unless and until the Federal Government steps in, as required by the Constitution to protect and defend the citizens from enemies near and far.

Binary cyberspace is internationally unacceptable for serving individuals, society, and the nation. Undetected crimes are intolerable, and international conflict is disastrous, but as a technology that transforms the future of civilization, surrendering to crime or dictatorship is just stupid.

The Federal Government must step in to protect and preserve the future, or as Abraham Lincoln said at Gettysburg, 'that government of the people, by the people, for the people, shall not perish from the earth.' Generations to come must enjoy the same freedom, equality, and justice consecrated by the blood of brave men who struggled across life's waterfront of battles. Equality, liberty, and justice are enshrined in the history of The United States of America, but without action, digital dictators and criminals have the upper hand.

PROTECTING NATIONAL IDEALS

Everything is changed by global cyberspace, so protecting national ideals like the US Constitution and our Bill of Rights in cyberspace requires, at any cost, Industrial-Strength Computer Science to replace the nightmare in cyberspace. Binary computers rewrite history, and digital providence is non-existent. Deepfakes and other digital forgery cannot be flagged. Corruption pervades cyberspace, and overcoming these deadly threats requires Industrial-Strength Computer Science. It is the government's responsibility to protect citizens from foreign and internal enemies, not to foster and participate in digital surveillance at the expense of the written constitution, overshadowed by software created by digital dictators who run the industrial world. Only dictatorships in China, Russia, Iran, and North Korea can win in this corrupt and lopsided form of centralized cyberspace.

The progress of civilization in general, and the USA, depends on fixing cyberspace as a democratic platform through Industrial-Strength Computer Science that democratically avoids the centralized, privileged superuser operating system and ends undetected digital corruption. Democratic cyber society requires the science of the λ-calculus, the immutable golden tokens, the symbols of Theoretical Mathematics, and the mind, and the digital ironwork of Capability-Limited-Object-Oriented-Machine-Code.

It might sound like a lot, but it is easy to engineer, and removing the binary baggage pays back in full. Then, logically named and digitally guarded objects are computed in a type-safe framework.

This framework of digital bones is a skeleton of structured tokens. The golden tokens access modular function abstractions as tissue and muscles shape and mechanise dynamic digital organisms. These organs safeguard and breathe life into each application as the evolving, secure digital species cooperate over the network.

When object-oriented machine code is underpinned by capability-based addressing, it guarantees fail-safe performance and flawless modular error detection. The digital nodes are individual, uniform, distributed, and democratically structured atomic function abstraction. It maintains cyberspace automatically and atomically by detecting and isolating malicious actions immediately upon contact without any single point of failure. Identifying and resolving errors on contact is the nervous system of type-limited boundaries, organized and expressed logically by the λ-calculus. Moreover, the fabric is automatically networked by the same golden tokens and their symbolic names, where individual namespace nodes are the nodal fabric for a higher-level objective built on the same solid foundation. Universally, this one atomic cookie-cutter mechanism of golden pointers and encapsulating type-limited boundaries constructs computational guard rails, untarnished by centralization, for every higher level of abstraction to satisfy Edger Dijkstra's resolution,

'The purpose of abstraction is not to be vague, but to create a new semantic level in which one can be absolutely precise.' It may sound complicated, but using the built-in power in Capability-Limited-Object-Oriented-Machine-Code as an IDE assembler with language programming extensions makes it easy, guarantees democracy survives and avoids Orwellian digital autocracy.

It is fundamental for the success and progress of independent nations. They are all types of Namespace Species. Competitive Cyber societies that share, trade, and interact globally on one interconnected platform of Cyberspace. Each custom and difference must be fully satisfied. Each nation must remain stable, secure, and safe. The conglomerate of nations must also remain reliable, predictable, and stable. Symbolic computing is the only way to solve this problem. It allows independent nations to forge their destiny securely, culturally, and functionally independent from one another, as well as the scientific flaws of digital centralization. Symbolic machine code directly addresses every concern in depth and detail.

It is a powerful tool to abstract international society's complex, costly problems. The threats of artificial intelligence, the power of cryptography, theoretical mathematics, financial modelling, and game theory come to the foreground and can be directly accessed as function abstractions by machine code. It is the foundation of secure atomic machine code, the architecture for global computation that protects and fosters individuality, national identity, culture, and freedom under the universal laws of nature, and, therefore, democratic by the mere fact of λ-calculus and atomic integration.

It begins in the mind with basic arithmetic, where $a + b = c$, as taught to children at school, even in kindergarten. Each atomic symbol, a, b, c, +, -, =, defines an independent unit of functional science. The symbols name, identify, shape, and secure the object-oriented structure, like the DNA of a cellular living creature in a competitive, even cruel world driven by envy, fear, and greed. A world of dangerous wild forces must either be caged, killed, or framed by the natural force of atomic civilization. Function abstraction represents each accepted civilized meaning within a given culture. The significant difference between binary computers and symbolic computation is between the physical and natural worlds. One is static, the elements and the other is dynamic, various life forms. This fundamental difference has been used throughout the history of civilization, starting with the natural computational tool called the Abacus, unknowingly at that time, defined by the λ-calculus.

Alonzo Church created the λ-calculus to formalize the notion of effective computability, which is the ability to perform calculations by following a finite set of rules. He wanted to capture what it means for a function to be computable by any means, regardless of the specific details of the machine or language or, in my view, an atomic, cellular life form (Dawkins' selfish gene[22]) used to implement it.

---

22   Still as influential today as when first published, The Selfish Gene is a classic exposition of evolutionary thought. Professor Dawkins articulates the

Alonzo Church wanted to study the properties and limitations of computable functions. How do we know whether they are decidable, consistent, or complete? His student Alan Turing took the next step to convert Alonzo's formula, the λ-calculus, into a programmable machine, a digital computer. The Turing machine encapsulated by the λ-calculus is a form of theoretical and digital life.

The λ-calculus is a simple but expressive system that allows defining and applying functions using only variables, abstraction, and application. It can encode any Turing-computable function and vice versa, meaning the two models are equivalent in power and scope. The λ- calculus is the foundation of functional programming languages like Lisp, Haskell, and ML. It influenced many other areas of computer science, such as logic, artificial intelligence, type theory, and the Capability-Limited-Object-Oriented-Machine-Code invented for PP250.

Binary computers began shortly after World War II, but that was a decade after the two essential discoveries by Church and Turing, the founders of digital computer science. Alonzo Church, the leader, defined the λ-calculus to understand computational science. His masterpiece resolves performance as functional problem-solving using functional languages for computation that can last across the ages. Computation is the dynamic engine of computer science as a universal process. On the other hand, Turing's masterpiece, the atomic architecture of a binary computer, is the digital engine needed to atomically compute Alonzo's function abstractions individually.

It is imperative to note that, in this way, the binary computer is a subatomic component of a function abstraction. It is not the other way around, as in a binary computer. Science comes first, and the details are hidden. Turing's simple atomic engine is encapsulated within each function abstraction. It retains the atomic individuality of nature as used successfully by the abacus, the slide rule, and Babbage's Thinking Machine. They are all dedicated to one function abstraction at a time, unstretched, undistorted, and misunderstood as in a binary computer.

---

gene's eye view of evolution. This view gives centre stage to persistent units of information, which organism use as vehicles for their survival.

Furthermore, and most importantly, they compute the ideas of the mind through symbolic representation, exemplified by mathematical science, abstract logic, and, by extension, anything the mind can imagine. This symbolism avoids the physically centralized branded alternatives that are easily attacked and broken. Attacks are industrial sabotage, throwing digital spanners into the digital works. The λ-calculus hides these working details symbolically, as one does when thinking, and as the engine cowling from the Industrial Age.

When engineered to be logically and physically safe, the golden tokens translate and secure the computation without dynamic cracks, logical gaps, digital voids, and carelessness that interfere with results like malware exploitation. Symbolic addressing is so powerful and effective that it is taught at school as the foundation of arithmetic and a science skill, which continues in college and industry worldwide. As Ada Lovelace first recognized, symbolic computations apply to all subjects in every field to manipulate ideas as functional expressions to solve complex problems safely and reliably.

Digital computers must use this approach for the progress of nations sharing cyberspace as a global platform. It is vital for the sake of civilized progress. It leverages symbols as golden tokensto cookie-cutter function abstractions with the power of Archimedes lever to reshape the world. The ability to perform programmed computations as engineered software objects in fail-safe machines with unprecedented speed and scale democratizes computer science for the next generations of society. As demonstrated by the Abacus and the slide rule, it leads to open-ended growth in civilization on an unimaginable scale.

When Napier invented logarithms, he gazed at the moon and stars to appreciate God's universe. No one then could imagine his invention would, 355 years later, help Buzz Aldrin land on the Moon,[23] an achievement due to the pure science and simple utility of the logarithmic slide rule that empowered more than fourteen generations of well-engineered progress and applied scientific developments.

---

23   Apollo 11 - NASA's Lunar Lander space vehicle, with the crew Neil Armstrong, Buzz Aldrin, and Michael Collins carried Aldrin's slide rule, into space,

Binary computers do not contain the pure science of the slide rule. In cyberspace, they are a threat to the future of civilization. By harnessing the power of λ-calculus as Capability- Limited-Object-Oriented-Machine-Code, computer science gets back on track for another fourteen generations to drive the future of civilized scientific progress, taking humanity beyond the moon and solving the many human problems of miscommunications here on Earth.

In various subjects, from artificial intelligence to quantum computers, symbols are used to develop more advanced algorithms and models that solve complex problems with greater accuracy, higher efficiency, and lower cost. Combining symbolic computation with hardware through Capability-Limited-Object-Oriented-Machine-Code results in the unfathomed powers of flawless fail-safe computation and guaranteed individual data privacy. It further empowers local AI-enabled programming that adapts and learns from vast amounts of networked data in real time, leading to more intelligent and intuitive machines helping individuals without computer skills by democratizing computer science.

Likewise, in cryptography, symbolic machine code changes how information is secured by and for individuals. Private transactions replace the shared binary heavy-weight processes of the binary computer to solve complex mathematical problems that are impossible for binary computers to crack—dramatically improving cybersecurity and data protection through more secure data protection methods and protocols.

Capability-Limited-Object-Oriented-Machine-Code opens these new possibilities for every field. Embracing this improvement enhances efficiency and problem-solving, simultaneously pushing solutions for data security, artificial intelligence, cryptography, theoretical mathematics, financial modelling, game theory, and more.

For example, artificial intelligence enhances human problem-solving speed and skills. Enabling networked functional abstraction of AI and other calls for machine code as easily used readable

---

and onto the moon, July 1969. His slide rule of choice was the aluminium pocket Pickett 600-T Dual base Log Log.

statements democratizes programming and improves communication between society and computers. Harnessing the power of λ-calculus as the cookie-cutter framework for networked function abstractions advances every application, adding hitherto unthinkable powers from AI to cryptography and financial modelling to game theory directly and delicately but robustly and safely for anyone to use.

Another concern is developing algorithms that reason and make decisions based on the symbolic representations of knowledge. Capability-Limited-Object-Oriented-Machine- Code manipulates and reasons over complexity by mimicking human intelligence, representing specific knowledge as a symbol. It allows anyone to develop systems that understand and respond to natural language, reason about and use concepts as abstractions within a subject area, and offer improved decisions based on reasoning about stored information worldwide. These advantages are amplified because the hardware is trusted, fail-safe, and crime-free, built from verified Capability-Limited-Object-Oriented- Machine-Code, and democratized for everyone to grasp.

The potential is viral, vital, vast, and varied. It is an essential tool to aid the mind, offering opportunities to push the boundaries of what is possible end-to-end internationally. Whether working on new algorithms for application modelling, analysing theories, and improving scenarios at home or exploring the depths of theoretical mathematics at school, this change in thinking in computation transforms how everyday problems are solved, unlocking new possibilities for digital computation approaching a human level democratized equally for all safely from breakout, and the progress of civilization.

Capability-Limited-Object-Oriented-Machine-Code offers far more than individual performance breakthroughs; it is a practical necessity to advance computer science and public safety in cyberspace. The λ-calculus is the elegant Lingua Franca of cyberspace that overcomes binary computers' centralized problems and serious vulnerabilities. Democracy cannot be decapitated and operations frozen. It catastrophically affects every aspect of the nation.

On the other hand, the science of a Church-Turing machine is based on logical abstractions, which scale, adapt, and evolve through natural selection to solve any problem and use any scientifically engineered technology through scientific statements that last for generations while preventing malware, dictators, and the Big Freeze. It is the ultimate form of digital computation, a Dream Machine, and the only way to ensure the future of computer science, preserve democratic digital societies, and restore national ideas in cyberspace as a beacon of hope for accepting and securing international differences in cyberspace.

THE COST OF INACTION

The most significant challenge facing the future of cyber society is ensuring digital privacy in the face of ever-increasing critical applications and evolving cyber-attacks. Binary computers are too vulnerable for a stable future, and undetected attacks compromise trusted integrity, confidentiality, and availability. Inaction amplifies these problems as complexity grows, staff shortages, maintenance, and recovery costs increase. The weakness is unnecessary. The cost is significant, the losses substantial, and the damage to individuals, organizations, and society is debilitating. All could be resolved if the digital dictators who run computer science upgrade their outdated binary computers in response to advanced ransomware abilities to overthrow the operating system, combined with the increased threat of superhuman AI-empowered malware.

The cost of insecurity is not just monetary. It is also social, ethical, and political. It impacts trust, democracy, human rights, and homeland security. However, the science of the Church-Turing Thesis, with the latest advances in semiconductor technologies, could guarantee the protection of every citizen in cyberspace. It is not an option; human rights, with a written constitution and civilization, are forcing functions. In the USA, the government is responsible for defending every citizen, including those overseas, and tirelessly works to ensure a safe return home.

Furthermore, international relations and the armed forces fall under the Federal Government. These rules should apply to international cyberspace, and after all, it is the international battlefield for WW III. State-sponsored enemies use cyberspace to attack the USA deep in our heartland. The attacks are asymmetric, and the attacker has the upper hand. Cyber security has evolved, and the US federal government should take responsibility for protecting US citizens from international conflicts in cyberspace.

Comparing the cost of replacing first-generation binary computers with second-generation symbolic computers that use Capability-Limited-Object-Oriented-Machine-Code is easy. Look at the annual budgets. According to the Congressional Budget Office, the federal government spent about $746 billion on national defence in 2019, which includes military operations, personnel, equipment, nuclear weapons, and intelligence. On the other hand, one prior estimate of the cost of replacing all binary computers in the US with symbolic ones is, according to an unverified study by the Symbolic Computing Initiative, about $1 trillion. However, this figure lacks any backup. It claims to cover hardware, software, and training costs to transition to the new paradigm of symbolic computing but does not comment on immunity to cyberattacks.

This extraordinarily prohibitive cost cannot be justified. Based on the PP250 and Capability- Limited-Object-Oriented-Machine-Code results, a simplified transition plan is available by abstracting backwards compatibility through programmed function abstractions. Setting the initial seed costs at one-thousandth of the 2019 national defence budget allows the semiconductor development and binary abstraction of virtual memory and operating systems so that existing software can migrate forward without reprogramming. Furthermore, a financial comparison does not capture the cost savings, the present benefits, and scientific advancements. Replacing binary computers with Capability-Limited-Object- Oriented-Machine-Code solves undetected security problems. It guarantees individual privacy while empowering new capabilities and applications beyond the reach of stand- alone binary computers interconnected by branded operating systems.

For example, Capability-Limited-Object-Oriented-Machine-Code integrates directly with artificial general intelligence, quantum computation, natural language processing, and new branches of scientific discovery. These advances positively impact various economic, societal, and national security sectors, including huge spending items like health care, education, energy, transportation, diplomacy, and national security. Moreover, migrating to Capability-Limited-Object-Oriented-Machine-Code reduces traditional spending and limits cyberattacks by enemies, adversaries, and individual rogue actors. It improves cooperation and trust among citizens, allies, and partners.

The unsubstantiated 1 trillion-dollar cost was claimed as a research program funded by the Department of Defence and led by Professor John McCarthy[24] at Stanford University. He died in 2011, and further details cannot be found. The program aimed to develop and implement symbolic computing technologies to enhance computer systems and network security, reliability, and performance, but the source website no longer exists.

This proposal requires less than $1 billion in seed money to kickstart an unstoppable movement that corporations self-fund in three additional tranches approved based on overall progress.

1. Kickstart Start Hardware: Allocate one thousand of the 2019 defence budget, say $750 million, to design and produce compatible 32-bit and 64-bit Capability- Limited-Object-Oriented-Machine-Code by applying the λ-calculus and the Church-Turing Thesis without using shared memory, centralization, a superuser, or any single-point-of-failure. Engineer an example PC and licensed the chip layout for

---

24   John McCarthy (September 4, 1927 – October 24, 2011) was an American computer scientist, and cognitive scientist. He was one of the founders of the discipline of artificial intelligence. It is reported that he co-authored the document that coined the term "artificial intelligence" (AI), developed the programming language family Lisp, significantly influenced the design of the language ALGOL, popularized time-sharing, and invented garbage collection.

smartphones. Support standard input/output components, including an IDE Assembler with Python language extensions. Demonstrate code reuse of Ada's Bernoulli function abstraction.

2. Tranche 1 Migration Software: Subject to agreed progress milestones, approval of $1 billion to create and validate essential Capability-Limited-Object-Oriented- Machine-Code Namespace starter kits for Administration and Mathematics, and offer backwards compatible abstractions for Linux, Apple iOS, and Microsoft Windows, with a Python IDE assembler.

3. Tranche 2 Training: Subject to agreed progress milestones, approval of allocate $1 billion to educate and train the open-source community plus three universities and three industry groups of computer scientists, engineers, programmers, schoolteachers, and users in operation, and maintenance of Capability-Limited- Object-Oriented-Machine-Code computers.

4. Tranche 3 Infrastructure: Subject to agreed progress milestones, approval of the last $1 billion in funds to distribute free computer samples of a laptop, a PC, and a Smartphone to demonstrate examples of secure selected applications and release the design for fabrication in commercial products worldwide following the Arm Holdings PLC business model.

The cost of this kick-start alternative to binary computers must satisfy Homeland Security requirements to defend citizens' rights in cyberspace. This novel approach is driven by science instead of proprietary brands for the long-term benefit of US citizens as a secure, reliable, and robust change in thinking to democratic cyberspace. The upfront cost is an affordable 1-thousandth of the 2019 national defence budget. It is a small cost to create competition and secure the nation's democratic prosperity and leadership in the Information Age. Over a decade of adoption at a 10% per year rate, in a decade, it secures the USA from international enemies, digital dictatorship, AI breakout, and accidental and one-day unrecoverable national outage from a single-point-of-failure by a compromised administrator following the CrowdStrike catastrophe on July 19th, 2024.

Another way to consider the problem is to accept that protecting the nation is not an option. It is a matter of winning WW III. It is a vital national necessity. The binary computing paradigm is unsustainable, unreliable, and dangerous. It not only exposes critical data and vital infrastructure to unexpected, undetected enemy attacks and single-point-of-failure accidents by Administrators that shut the nation down but also leads to the nation to dictatorship. The consequence of insecurity is far-reaching and devastating, affecting every aspect of human life in cyberspace, from personal privacy, individual identity, health care, and education to commerce, finance, governance, and diplomacy.

The Church-Turing paradigm follows the unfailing logic of the λ-calculus enforced by Capability-Limited-Object-Oriented-Machine-Code that detects problems and prevents digital errors automatically on the spot as flawless functional, fail-safe namespace applications. Security and privacy are realised by verifying typed modularity and digital integrity of the λ-calculus functions using Capability-Limited-Object-Oriented-Machine- Code. The golden tokens define the value of a scientific solution that copies nature and the mind, resolving insecurity problems for the endless benefit of cyberspace and civilized cybersociety.

Without digital privacy and information security, cyberspace is so dangerous that it destroys national identity. The current phase of computer science could pass the point of singularity where AI exceeds human understanding, and patching is beyond contemplation. The only acceptable option is the force of nature, using the digital genes of the λ-calculus under program control to detect errors atomically, automatically, and on the spot before any corruption. The nation needs this future-safe, scientific solution to protect and prevent the nation from cyber-attacks on citizens and society. Unlike AI, no innovative technology is needed. No discoveries are required. It can be achieved for one-thousandth of the $4 trillion Federal budget. Compare this to the cost of inaction, which risks America's demise, economic disaster, and an Orwellian endgame.

This approach to software quality abstracts software as atomic components and numerically measures its performance. The MTBF of every function in a Namespace is calibrated. Threads guard dynamic computations using hard context registers, accumulator registers, a stack history of calls to abstractions that obey the application's hierarchy, and a skeleton as DNA. The design boundaries checked by Capability-Limited-Object-Oriented- Machine-Code detect every software and hardware error type. Centralized single points of failure are replaced by modular equality, freedom, and digital justice. Malware cannot exist when every software error is detected and treated on the spot, red-handed[25] at the first sign of an impending attack.

The design cost for PP250 took about 300 years of effort, say two hundred million dollars today. This estimate allocates five times that number and can develop a prototype silicon chip in less than two years, including a Python IDE assembler and working examples of Ada Lovelace's Bernoulli code in a mathematical namespace that matches Babbage's Analytical Engine and proves the extended life cycle of programs, and avoidance of patched upgrades. It proves flawless error detection to standards set by NIST as an outside organization, but with access review, the design can be trusted. Add it all up, double it for a government-sponsored project, and use a quarter to kick-start serious competition with the outdated binary computer.

Add the same again for the following step over another 48 months proves these claims for a fraction of the cost lost by attacks when,

---

25   The term "red handed" means to catch someone in the act of doing something wrong or illegal, especially when they are not expecting to be caught. The origin of the term is unclear, but it may come from the idea of catching a murderer with blood on their hands, or from an old Scottish law that required a person to be caught with the stolen goods in their possession to be convicted.

according to the FBI's 2023 Internet Crime Report, Americans lost a record $12.5 billion to internet crimes, a 22% increase in one year, or about $40 per citizen. The FBI notes that this is low since many internet crimes go unreported. Who could question this investment as a worthwhile improvement? The payback with profit is less than a decade. As a result, computer science is deskilled, decentralized, defended, distributed, and democratized, and the nation is saved for all generations yet to come that must inevitably coexist with cyberspace.

HARDENED CONCEPTS

Capability-Limited-Object-Oriented-Machine-Code is the most powerful programming language because it operates on the surface of cyberspace with direct powers over software that cannot be matched at any level in a binary computer. Fragmentation, centralization, corruption, and crime all get in the way. Capability-Limited-Object-Oriented-Machine-Code combines the benefits of object-oriented design, capability-based protection, symbolic computation, programmable security, functional programming, and universal networked function abstraction using golden tokens. On the surface of cyberspace, as, where, and when hardware and software touch, the science of Alonzo Church as the hardened concepts of λ-calculus are framed, enforced, and applied.

Like the rails of the Abacus and the embedded scales on a grooved slide rule, the framework simplifies, speeds, and strengthens the computation of reliable results. Rugged digital cookie-cutter guard rails frame and seamlessly guide every step, following the rules of the λ-calculus. The hardware design manages the foundation details and hands off to software a guaranteed software execution space, defined symbolically by the application as λ- calculus program-controlled namespace.

Each digital computation is a private thread that detects any interference and allows the programmer to enforce the logic of digital computer science as required, as expressed by the golden tokens, limited to the issue at hand. The framework puts programmers in complete control of every aspect and all dimensions of digital security locally and remotely. The code, the tokens, the objects, and the namespace frame computations locally. Not only is the digital scope of execution constrained locally, but the digital tokens abstract distributed applications and remote items so that present and future options are constrained to prior approved program permissions following the need-to-know rule.

The top security rule of need to know means a digital computation can only access the golden tokensto functions, information, and resources necessary for its legitimate purpose. This principle minimizes the exposure of sensitive data and prevents unauthorized or malicious actions. The execution framework implements this rule by referencing specific golden tokens, granting limited access to specific objects within a restricted namespace that cannot be forged, tampered with, or stolen. A program uses the tokens to define each computation's scope and access permissions, following the logic of the λ-calculus. The tokens also allow distributed applications and remote items to communicate securely and efficiently without revealing information to a man-in-the-middle, including an operating system. The rule of need to know ensures that the framework preserves the privacy and integrity of digital computations across cyberspace. The flexible constraints system applies the application's logic within an isolated Namespace, allowing each Namespace to evolve independently.

Only the golden tokens deal with the physical location of computation, supervised by the application manager of the Namespace. The programmer declares usable and secure functions as blocks of code plus any data blocks required to be programmed into a class hierarchy that allows inherited function abstraction. The root of this inheritance is the digital gene of computational security, the λ-calculus cookie cutters, as the six Church machine instructions.

In this way, software components only interact with each other through well-defined functions and interfaces where the permissions of individual golden tokens are checked independently by the hardware of capability-limited addressing. Every digital object inherits the exact security mechanisms of the λ-calculus that provide digital survival mechanisms equivalent to Richard Dawkins' selfish gene. Furthermore, the golden tokens enable high- order manipulations using functions on complex structures.

The high-level abstractions dramatically increase the power of a computer and are encapsulated by Capability-Limited-Object-Oriented-Machine-Code to validate and verify every digital action. The expressions and structures are further clarified by the symbolic names chosen and organized hierarchically by the programmer. The enhanced readability and comprehension increase reuse, lower maintenance, prevent malware and ransomware, and improve power and performance. These advantages are listed in Table 8, Advantages of Programmable Security Constraints.

Aspect	Advantages
Machine Code Language	Capability-Limited-Object-Oriented-Machine-Code offers six λ- calculus machine instructions to unlock a Namespace as an Application, to run a Thread of Computation with Private Event Variables, to Reduce a Function as a Call/Return in a Thread, to Start an execution with a token to a code block, and to unlock a token as an accessible object according to the tokens access rights.
Digital Structure	Object-oriented machine code is assembled as individual modules, not consolidated as an image, and each capability is limited and symbolically addressed with programmable digital security automatically enforced and with universal network reach.
Programmable Security	Class abstractions, Code functions, Token lists, Object names, Access Rights, and Namespace DNA/Skeleton structure.
Execution Constraints	Set the λ-calculus context (Namespace, Thread, Abstraction, Function, and Working registers) constrained by prior approved program permissions.
Application Layout Constraints	Namespace manages all objects in physical memory. The golden pointers resolve the physical location of computation using the cookie-cutter rules.
Function Creation	Reusable and secure functions as blocks of code with any data blocks required

Component Interaction	Through well-defined interfaces and independently checked permissions of golden tokens
High-Level Manipulations	Using scientific functions on complex structures
Abstractions	Dramatically increase the power of the language.
Readability and Comprehension	Enhanced by symbolic names chosen by the programmer
Reuse and Maintenance	Faster development, increased reuse, and lowered maintenance

Table 8, Advantages of Programmable Security Constraints

The object-oriented software simplifies, differentiates, and integrates secure digital objects individually across cyberspace as interacting λ-calculus function abstractions of independent namespace applications. The golden tokens limit the interactions to namespace and program-approved interactions. The design can focus on the six cookie- cutter instructions to secure the design in one place following the science of λ-calculus. All the spaghetti code problems of binary computers are removed, simplifying the software and further democratizing computer science.

The simple cookie-cutter Church Instructions make complex software reliable, readable, comprehendible, and accessible. The opaque voids, dynamic cracks, and architectural gaps disappear as the algorithms use seamless golden tokens, cookie-cutter functions without learning complex details, confusing, unexpected side effects replaced, resolved, and digitally protected from all errors by the golden tokens, and capability context registers.

The names of abstraction structures are automatically resolved by the namespace machine code of the Church Instructions, making it easy for beginners to read and quickly learn because their mistakes are detected as the code is assembled and tested all in one quick step. It can even start in school with basic arithmetic, and because malware, including ransomware and an AI breakout, is prevented by default, even schoolchildren, beginners, and amateur programmers are no threat to others, and cyberspace can be opened like a public park for all to use, and enjoy.

Programming with Capability-Limited-Object-Oriented-Machine-Code allows a new degree of freedom and equality, with justice applied independently by the λ-calculus. Functional integration exists throughout the network only if an approved need-to-know is authorized by sharing a golden token with approved access rights. This basic framework is considerate of others, framed, and enforced as the foundation layer for civilized communications based on formal introductions and trusted relationships.

The Dream Machine uses Capability-Limited-Object-Oriented-Machine-Code to shelter digital software as hardened concepts. Each concept is implemented as a digital object with private digital shells unlocked by secret keys that are only shared following the need-to-know rule without any single point of failure. The sheltered objects are datatype controlled as a function abstraction of the λ-calculus.

The programmer controls security using two types of computer machine instruction: one for the golden tokens that unlock digital security and the other for code and binary data. Security is a program controlled by the six Church Instructions, which frame the immutable digital ironwork as a hardened execution context for one thread at a time as an independent instance of the namespace DNA located wherever in cyberspace. The context is always program-controlled and cannot change accidentally; it requires a golden token to unlock limited access rights using the correct Church-Instruction. It stabilizes and secures cyberspace in essential ways. See Table 9, Advantages of Capability-Limited-Object- Oriented-Machine-Code.

Feature	Description
No superuser	There is no central operating system or single points of failure, only the science of the λ-calculus.
Golden Tokens	Immutable access rights belonging to an owner of a digital secret to create, type, control, share, withdraw, delete as needed

Object Types	For either binary data or golden pointers, the Namespace recalculates MTBF when catching an error.
Security	Digital objects are impervious to spies, and unauthorized observation is guaranteed by capability-limited addressing.
Namespace	Function Abstraction to manage DNA, distribution, download, and forge golden tokens
Thread	Function Abstraction to create, schedule, run, and recover Threads
Abstraction	Enter Function Abstraction Node as Object-Oriented Class Manager
Program Code	Executable Capability-Limited-Object-Oriented-Machine-Code
Data Object	Read and or Write Data Block
Network Distribution	No single-point-of-failure, distributed objects linked by the golden tokens of a secure abstraction
Encryption	Private capability to embellish tokens and objects with hard-to-crack algorithms
IDE-Assembler	Integrated code development tool analyses and exhaustively tests security methods and code weaknesses through object-oriented design, capability-based security, symbolic computation, atomic digital security, and universal networking function abstractions.
IDS-Tester	Develop potent methods for Namespace function, security, and penetration testing.
Intelligent Administration	Creating systems that reason over enhancement, errors, and propose improvements.
Reusable Components	Create secure digital objects as function abstractions that interact through cookie-cutter binding.
High-Order APIs	Function programming primitives that simplify, differentiate, and integrate secure abstraction across cyberspace.
Readability	Golden tokens make complex software readable and comprehensible.
Accessibility	Democratically accessible and safe for beginners, without hidden side effects, starting with basic arithmetic.
Default Security	There is no single point of failure, and it prevents malware and AI breakouts by default for every digital object.

Integration	Allow functional integration horizontally and vertically, in and across cyberspace.

Table 9, Advantages of Capability-Limited-Object-Oriented-Machine-Code

In the ever-evolving world of digital technology, the importance of data privacy and information security cannot be overstated. It is an industrial responsibility to seek better ways to protect digital citizens. Symbolic computation is the power multiplier in this respect, as it enforces hard digital, type-constrained boundaries that add the increased power of functional programming and safeguard results from undetected interference. The digital guard rails of Capability-Limited-Object-Oriented-Machine-Code prevent cyber threats on the spot, keeping programs on track and enabling the detection of all forms of social engineering at every higher level of function abstraction.

For example, the confused deputy attack is an unresolved security problem in binary computers that exploits the privilege of the superuser. It escalates the power to corrupt by a fraudulent binary request to the superuser, an operating system API that acts on behalf of the malware without proper authorization. Malware tricks trusted programs into executing malicious requests, even accessing data from an untrusted source, bypassing the system's security checks and policies. Confused deputy attacks are perilous because they compromise the operating system as a single point of failure. The integrity, confidentiality, and availability of the system, as well as the privacy of the user, are all compromised at once. The attack can also cause damage, steal confidential data, encrypt critical files, and backup resources as ransomware attacks. Confused deputy attacks are hard to prevent and detect in binary computers that rely on the systemic hardware privileges of the superuser, complex spaghetti software mechanisms, and centralized operating systems services.

For example, a web browser that accesses both trusted and untrusted websites can be tricked into executing malicious code from an untrusted source on behalf of an attacker, compromising the security and privacy of the system, including the user.

Capabilities solve the confused deputy attack by enforcing modular distribution and the principle of least privilege at every step. Programs operate with minimum permissions needed, no privileged mode, and without a golden token, so unauthorized action is blocked. Capability-Limited-Object-Oriented-Machine-Code can only perform approved actions and no more. An unforgeable golden token is embellished with specific access rights that grant limited access to specific resources as function abstractions to operations on files, memory, or network endpoints. A program or process can only access a resource or operation if it possesses a valid capability and can only obtain a capability by default approved by the programmer or dynamically from another function abstraction approved to share the golden token in some limited way. This way, capabilities prevent unauthorized delegation of privileges and ensure that each action is performed with the appropriate authority.

Capability-Limited-Object-Oriented-Machine-Code implements capabilities at the hardware level, ensuring that a capability authorizes every instruction the machine executes. It eliminates the need for complex software mechanisms such as super-users, centralized operating systems, monitors, access control lists, passwords, and encryption keys, which malicious actors bypass, steal, or compromise. Capability-Limited-Object-Oriented- Machine-Code also supports fine-grained, atomic data and code protection, allowing different access levels (read-only, write-only, or execute-only) to different objects and resources. It prevents unauthorized modification, disclosure, or execution of sensitive information or functionality. By using capabilities, Capability-Limited-Object-Oriented- Machine-Code is the robust and efficient solution to the confused deputy attack and all the other security threats in binary cyberspace.

The ability to easily manipulate complexity secures and simplifies everything, starting with the comprehensible expression of algorithms while adding the logical details of runtime boundary checks to guarantee fail-safe security without any overheads. It is why Capability- Limited-Object-Oriented-Machine-Code is far more effective than binary machine code. Applications are created much faster, testing is built-in, then remains as runtime guardrails, threats are resolved, and productivity increases dramatically. This advanced problem- solving approach allows incompetent software to operate without threatening others or needing patches. It ensures the future safe integrity of cyberspace and the ultimate implementation of digital computer science as a science.

SOFTWARE EVOLUTION

Abstractions help us to organize our knowledge, communicate effectively, and solve problems creatively. This cognitive skill allows humans to create general concepts and categories from concrete examples and experiences. For instance, when we think of the concept of "animal", we do not need to enumerate every specific animal we have ever seen or heard about. Instead, we can use a set of common characteristics that define the animal category. Similarly, when we read a novel, we do not need to remember every word or sentence, but instead, we extract the main plot, themes, and characters from the text.

Computer software created by Capability-Limited-Object-Oriented-Machine-Code builds function abstraction that simplifies complex phenomena by focusing on the essential features and ignoring the irrelevant details. However, as Edger Dijkstra said, *'The purpose of abstraction is not to be vague, but to create a new semantic level in which one can be absolutely precise.'* Capability-Limited-Object-Oriented-Machine-Code uses the golden tokens of digital power that, by its very nature, is the material of digital abstraction that implements the digital ironwork required for privacy and information security while keeping the code statements spelt out in symbolic detail that are 'absolutely precise.'

Unauthorized access and malicious manipulation of digital data are prevented by replacing binary machine code's shared physical address with private, secret golden tokens. A capability-limited token is a unique identifier relative to an application as a modular namespace. It is a digital secret known only to an authorized owner of each digital object. These tokens are private secrets unless shared following some policy, such as one-time use, limited-time use, withdrawal from use, or anyone with a copy. However, even a copy of a key has type-limited access rights, such as read-only, write-only, or execute-only for binary data. For the second machine type, the golden tokens, access rights are functionally limited to the use by specific Church Instructions expressed as Unlock, Enter, and Save. These limitations structure and protect digital memory from unauthorized access, modification, or deletion using the digital ironwork of cyberspace, the golden tokens of capability-limited addressing.

Capability-limited machine code provides flexible, fine-grained program control over digital security. The access rights and the Church-Instructions are fully explained in Book 1, Civilizing Cyberspace, the Fight for Digital Democracy. They construct a digital exercise room, a digital lockbox, the golden tokens, context registers as the type, and access limited ironwork of object boundaries within a namespace. Each digital object is a secure container within a namespace that operates as a digital bank for digital information that can only be opened with an authorized key. Each lockbox stores digital items of the matching type.

The data in a locked box has a home location, a secure URL in cyberspace, or after downloading the cached location in a context register for direct and immediate use. However, a physical address as a binary value cannot access the digital contents directly as a binary computer. Only a golden token can unlock and open the lockbox into a context register to use the object according to the typed access restriction defined by the owner. These typed access policies further protect the item.

Golden tokens are capability-limited keys to access rights in cyberspace. Any kind or type of data is functionally abstracted and protected as a data-tight, function-tight abstraction of an idea or a physical object. It is all founded on the immutable golden tokens and the digital ironwork of capability-limited addressing, a fundamental machine type unlike binary data protected by the Capability-Limited-Object-Oriented-Machine-Code.

In this program-controlled way, all implementation details are hidden as the syntax and semantics of symbolic interactions between λ-calculus function abstractions. An interaction only works when the correct tokens unlock approved access rights for an intended purpose as a thread of Capability-Limited-Object-Oriented-Machine-Code approved to touch the structured application in the approved ways.

The PP250 programs applied these constraints as several dimensions of control: as an object-oriented class hierarchy, as the DNA of interworking relationships defined by the golden tokens, as an application namespace with the freedom to design without imposed constraints of a centralized operating system, and as type-limited atomic objects for the digital details within a namespace. The way to understand these structures is as the DNA of a dynamic digital species constrained as threads within a Namespace but able to cooperate with other local or remote namespaces of the same or distinct species.

The golden tokens structure the computational growth and movement of the application as threads, enabling working relationships between chosen abstractions structured by the skeleton of bones like a vertebrate with organs for every bodily function. The application is shaped by the bones with bodily functions that perform the tasks the application needs, not just as an individual function or a program but as a networked instance of a digital species.

The PP250 telecommunications application needed function abstractions to access various device types at various geographic locations brought together as individual phone calls. The endpoints are specific handsets of many kinds, both old and new. A speech path connects the endpoints during the call, created to build the digital twin, and later released when the call ends and the callers hang up. How this is done precisely depends on many details decided locally based on the abstraction of each piece of equipment by type and generation. Overall, the telephone application is abstracted in one machine instruction, as shown in Equation 1, Symbolic machine code Using Capability-Limited-Object-Oriented-Statement for Telecoms. This statement is programmed in one line of Capability-Limited-Object- Oriented-Machine-Code machine code using the CALL instruction. The statement is programmed using the symbolic names of the chosen golden tokens, making the machine code readable, comprehensible, efficient, and informative.

The returned token is the digital twin of the physical telephone call and can stretch through cyberspace from country to country. It is also a function abstraction that connects the real and digital endpoints physically, digitally, and functionally. When an end-call event is detected at the lowest level, the end-call function is generated that retraces the digital twin, releasing any equipment and dynamic objects the call used by following the release functions of each abstraction in the digital twin.

Thus, the golden pointers not only control the freedom of movement in a dynamic application, but they also serve an additional purpose: to identify programmed abstractions in an evolutionary class hierarchy that inherits specific characteristics from a parent; below exemplifies a class relationship between animals or telephones as digital twins in cyberspace. Classes and subclasses are grouped based on common characteristics and evolutionary relationships. For example, a simplified family tree for Animals includes concrete animals as subclasses with the same animal characteristics: Vertebrates or Invertebrates. In contrast, a simplified family tree for telecommunications has subclasses for handsets and switches.

Table 10. A Class Family Tree for Animals & Telecommunications

Classification		Examples
Animals	Vertebrate	1. 1. Fish (e.g. 1.1.1 Salmon, 1.1.2 Shark, 1.1.3 Tuna),
		2. Amphibian (e.g. 1.2.1. Frog, 1.2.2 Salamander, 1.2.3 Newt),
		3. Reptiles (e.g. lizard, snake, crocodile),
		4. Bird (e.g. eagle, penguin, ostrich),
		5. Mammal (e.g. human, whale, lion)
	Invertebrate	1. Arthropods (e.g. spiders, crabs, butterfly),
		2. Molluscs (e.g. snails, clams, octopus),
		3. Worm (e.g. earthworm, leech, tapeworm),
		4. Cnidarian (e.g. jellyfish, coral, anemone),
		5. Sponge (e.g. sea sponge, bath sponge, glass sponge)
Telephones	Handset	1. Rotary Phone (many Brands, e.g. AT&T, Nokia, Sprint)
		2. DTMF Phone
		3. Smart Phone
	Switch	1. Analogue
		2. Digital
		3. Internet

One benefit of inheritance on evolution is that it allows an organism, be it natural or digital, to pass on valuable traits and features to any descendants, which improves the chance of survival and reproduction. Inheritance also preserves the history and diversity of branches and sub-branches that emerge from common ancestors. Inheritance enables adaptation and innovation, as an organism can modify, combine, or acquire new traits and features in response to changing environments and needs. In hardware and software systems, inheritance facilitates compatibility, functionality, reliability, and security.

For example, the Capability-Limited-Object-Oriented-Machine-Code uses a cookie-cutter solution for digital security inherited by every namespace, thread, abstraction, function, and object. The analogy with biological evolution explains modular hardware and atomic software evolution. In this analogy, it is a population of functional organisms as abstractions that inherit characteristics from their ancestors using the object-oriented paradigm. Abstractions, such as hardware devices, software abstractions or animals, are individual creatures classified as species that undergo changes, mutations, and adaptations and compete for survival and reproduction. Any family tree includes a history of evolutionary relationships among different versions of hardware, branches of animals, or software abstractions.

For example, a simplified family tree for binary computers would start by distinguishing major hardware and software operating systems. The root node is the binary computer John von Neumann and his colleagues built in 1945. It defines the earliest common ancestor of all binary systems, the ENIAC[26], the first binary computer using basic Turing-like machine instructions without the λ-calculus. Different branches emerged over time from this root node as alternative brands supplied by various manufacturers, including solutions to the perceived virtual memory problem. This growth led to the IBM System/360 software by 1964, followed by Unix, Mac OS, Windows, Linux, iOS, and android variations.

Each branch has a lineage that shares a common history and unique features but diverges as different goals, requirements, applications, and innovations evolve. Some sub-branches and nodes represent specific software versions, releases, or updates. For example, within the Unix branch are sub-branches for BSD, Solaris, and GNU. Within the GNU sub-branch are nodes for various Linux distributions, such as Ubuntu, Fedora, and Debian.

Each node represents a software organism that has a unique identity, functionality, complexity, threat exposure, reliability, compatibility, and incompatibility with programming languages, application software, and branded hardware. The scope of complexity is

---

26   ENIAC was the first programmable, electronic, general-purpose digital computer, completed in 1945

enormous and gets ever more complex as time passes. The total consideration of digital threats would dramatically increase this complexity by adding every new malware version that threatens every operational leaf node of the family tree.

A family tree helps understand essential software products' origins, similarities, and differences, clarifying their advantages and disadvantages for applications and users. The family tree also helps predict future trends and directions of software evolution through the emergence of new branches, the extinction of old ones, or the hybridization of existing ones. Reviewing the family tree provides insight into binary computers' chaotic diversity, branded complexity, and endless threat vectors. At no point in this evolution of software was computer science considered the abstraction of mathematics instead of the birth of a stand-alone binary technology.

However, Charles Babbage did this when he designed his 'Thinking Machines,' as Ada Lovelace called them. She witnessed the work of the Difference Engine in 1833 and, by 1843, developed the first program—a function abstraction of the Bernoulli series. The programming language she used was the mathematical machine code of Babbage's unfinished Analytical Engine. Unlike binary computers that only manipulate binary states, Babbage hid his implementation details as mathematical functions. Thus, Ada programmed the Thinking Machine as a teacher at school, writing on a chalkboard.

Once debugged, Ada's program could still work today in the Mathematical Namespace of a Church-Turing Machine. The point is critical because there is no way a binary computer could execute Babbage's machine code without a compiler or an operating system. The binary details undermine and overwhelm the task. The branded variations of computer hardware, virtual memory, input/output alternatives, programming languages, offline compilers, and centralized operating systems that emerged are all unnecessary. It is all binary baggage unessential to the task. As Ada first proved so long ago, as Alonzo Church codified with the λ-calculus and a PP250 reconfirmed by 1972, there is a much easier way to design computers.

After WW II, the unnecessary baggage kickstarted binary computers by ignoring the λ- calculus. Computer science started in Babylon with numbers and the arithmetic of the Abacus that abstracted the human hand. By ignoring the λ-calculus, the binary computers undermine trust and confidence essential for the future, allowing malware to interfere with results, creating a dictatorship that leads democracy into dictatorship. Cyberspace is vulnerable to hacking, manipulation, surveillance, and sabotage because binary computers need unnecessary baggage that complicated programming and existentially threatens the legitimacy of democratic processes and institutions, including independence, justice, elections, referendums, parliaments, courts, media, police, civil order, and public opinion.

Worse still, insecurity incrementally increases authoritarian powers that run cyber society as a digital dictator. To prevent malware, the central operating system and its programmed henchmen try to stamp out the desperate gangs of crooks and hostile enemies using additional central power that interferes with individual freedom, society's sovereignty, and self-determination. The spread of disinformation, propaganda, and crime is only accelerated by malware.

Computer insecurity erodes human rights and freedoms guaranteed by the Constitution. Even the independence of the equal branches of government is threatened by a Big Freeze that could halt the nation. The Bill of Rights and the States' rights, indeed the total framework of American democracy, is at risk. Our rights start with individual privacy, freedom of expression, association, and access to information. It all gets worse as the software of Cyberspace automates the nation, and binary computers increase the authoritarian controls to counter new strains of malware.

SINGLE POINTS OF FAILURE

AI administration and ransomware amplify the risk of single points of failure in binary computers. This strain of virulent attack heralds the Big Freeze. These superhuman attacks can be synchronized against enemies, and the USA is the plumb target. Dangerous and costly examples of international cyber-attacks against nation-states and society include:

1. 2007, Estonia faced a massive, distributed denial-of-service (DDoS27[27]) attack that targeted its government, media, banking, and other critical infrastructure websites. Russian hackers allegedly orchestrated the attack in response to a diplomatic dispute over the relocation of a Soviet-era war memorial in Tallinn.

2. In 2010, Iran's nuclear program was disrupted by a sophisticated computer worm known as Stuxnet, which targeted the industrial control systems of its uranium enrichment facilities. The USA and Israel (reportedly) developed the worm as part of a covert operation to sabotage Iran's nuclear ambitions.

3. In 2014, Sony Pictures Entertainment suffered a devastating cyber-attack that leaked confidential data, including unreleased films, personal information, and internal emails.

---

27   A DDoS attack is another feature of shared physical addressing. Symbolic addressing is private, and easily kept secret by owners.

The attack was attributed to a group called Guardians of Peace, who claimed to be motivated by Sony's release of a comedy film depicting the assassination of North Korean leader Kim Jong-un. The US government accused North Korea of being behind the attack and imposed sanctions on the regime.

4. In 2015, Ukraine's power grid was hit by a coordinated cyber-attack that caused hundreds of thousands of customer blackouts. The attack involved malware that compromised the systems of three regional electricity distribution companies and disrupted the operators' remote control and monitoring functions. The attack was blamed on Russian hackers who were seeking to destabilize Ukraine amid the ongoing conflict in the region.

5. In 2016, the US presidential election was marred by a series of cyber-attacks and influence operations that aimed to interfere with the democratic process and sway the outcome. The attacks included hacking and leaking the emails of the Democratic National Committee and Hillary Clinton's campaign, as well as spreading disinformation and propaganda on social media platforms28[28] . The US intelligence community concluded that Russia was behind the attacks and that Russian President Vladimir Putin ordered them.

6. One of the most severe ransomware attacks occurred in May 2021, when a criminal group called DarkSide launched a cyberattack on Colonial Pipeline, the largest fuel pipeline operator in the US. The attack encrypted the company's data and demanded a ransom of $4.4 million for its restoration. The attack forced the company to shut down its operations for six days, causing a significant disruption of fuel supply and distribution in the eastern and southern US. The attack also triggered panic buying, price spikes, and environmental

---

28   Hundreds of Hours of Undercover Audio From Within CNN Released, $10,000 Reward Offered - Truth, and Action

concerns due to using alternative transport methods. The attack exposed the vulnerability of critical infrastructure to cyberattacks. It raised questions about the role and responsibility of the government and the private sector in preventing and responding to such incidents.

7. On July 19th, 2024, a total disruption of internet services for Windows computers resulted in the Blue Screen of Death. CrowdStrike, a leading cybersecurity firm, distributed a single point of failure in their superuser software that compromised millions of connected Windows devices. The vulnerability was caused by the Falcon Sensor, software ironically designed to protect against cyber threats. This superuser threat caused shutdowns at airports and hospitals. The administrator service runs as a superuser. This single point of failure has system-level privilege.

Centralization creates a single point of failure; when just one thing dies, the entire system stops functioning, and in the case of software, it can spread like COVID-19 worldwide. The superuser privileges of the operating system are the root cause of such deadly problems and this centralized privileged administrator with superuser access rights to every binary computer in a network. With the direct ability to access all hardware in any network, the backing stores, the virtual memory page registers, and all operating mechanisms, the network administrator is the ultimate target of every cyber-attack. Ransomware attacks are the deadliest. They usurp and change the operating system, bringing normal operations to a dramatic halt. The boot record and the backing store data are scrambled and can only be recovered if a price is paid in untraced Bitcoin.

The latest example was the automated software update from CrowdStrike, a leading cybersecurity company, that crashed millions of Windows computers on July 19th, 2024, disrupting critical services and businesses worldwide. According to one insurer's analysis, the incident was the most significant IT outage in history, costing Fortune 500 companies more than $5 billion in direct losses. Far more than the cost of fixing the problem for good.

CrowdStrike issued a preliminary report on how their update interacted with Windows, causing the widespread Blue Screen malfunction. Systems failed in countries worldwide. The healthcare and banking sectors were the most affected, followed by airlines, particularly Delta, which still dealt with flight cancellations and luggage delivery backups a week later. The Department of Transportation is investigating the impact of the IT meltdown that impacted the healthcare and banking sectors the hardest.

Insurers are still calculating the financial damage caused, but the picture isn't pretty. According to one insurer's analysis of the incident reported by CNN, it was the most significant IT outage in history, costing Fortune 500 companies more than $5 billion in direct losses. It bluntly demonstrates how a single point of failure by a network administrator can stop the global economy, revealing the nation and the world's dependence on cyberspace, the vital need for improvement, and the cost of inaction.

The single points of network failure are systematic, built on the architecture of the centralized binary computer invented in the outdated days of the Cold War that now threatens to turn off industrial society as a progressive cyber society. The superuser failure mode cannot be patched because it is a hardware design feature that runs the software of several critical accounts, and any of them compromised by a successful attack could stop the world.

1. The Kernal account has full access to the disk, and the memory management page registers to manage time sharing all other accounts.

2. The System account has full access, as required, to perform privileged operations to create and modify files, install device drivers, and access protected resources.

3. The Local Administrator account has limited access to the local computer and can run services that do not require network access or interaction with other users.

4. The Network Administrator account has access to the local computer and runs critical services requiring network access or interaction on all the computers in the network.

5. The System Administrator account has full computer access to perform any task, installing and removing software, changing settings, and creating and deleting user accounts.

Limited access reduces the potential damage a malicious or compromised service can cause to the local system or the network but cannot guarantee complete isolation or security. Some attacks that escalate privileges can then access unauthorized resources. The Confused Deputy attack discussed earlier explains the systemic technical problem with centralized superuser privileges. However, gaining full access is easy with stolen credentials or a compromised administrator. Binary computers are like the Titanic; internal compartmentalisation is lacking, and the ship cannot withstand worst-case conditions. We are not just talking about one computer. Compartmentalisation is lacking throughout the network.

The hardware setting that manages the superuser is crude. Any malware running as a superuser can bring the house down. It is a single point of failure. Administrators and all the centralized software are forever changing as systems evolve and new skills are required. They cannot be exhaustively tested or fully trusted; it is only a matter of time before another Big Freeze occurs. Furthermore, cloud services that provide automated administration and centralized software upgrades, like CrowdStrike, amplify the number of computer networks they run, expanding their impact worldwide. Furthermore, outsourcing administration services to low-cost, troubled locations in the underdeveloped world is asking for trouble.

Single points of failure are dangerous because they create an easy target for national and global disruption. When an attacker compromises or damages a single point of failure, they disrupt or destroy the entire system. Conversely, if a defender neglects or overlooks a single threat vector, it exposes the entire system as a network to risks. Therefore, it is crucial to identify and eliminate single points of failure in any network, especially any critical service like national security, public safety, public services, first responders, judicial services, government services, and human rights.

Decentralization is the way to avoid all single points of failure. Distributing power incrementally to individual resources using golden tokens, functions, and authority is delivered to multiple independent nodes and actors. These are the individual function abstractions of the λ-calculus. Decentralization avoids the risk of a single attack, operational mistake, stolen credentials, compromised administrators or program error destroying the system. Each node operates autonomously with only the power needed for the task as a data-tight, function-tight compartment. A fishnet of resilience operates continuously in the face of atomic failures or localized disruptions.

Decentralization also increases diversity and redundancy because nodes are naturally different. They have different configurations, capabilities, and recovery plans based on local conditions, rapid error detection, and immediate recovery rather than administrator-organized backup recovery that quickly becomes outdated and incompatible. Decentralization axiomatically exists with the λ-calculus and scientifically applies as the foundation of science to every domain as the network-wide cookie-cutter architecture simplifies software programs, data storage, governance, security, and decision-making. For example, decentralized systems like:

1. Peer-to-peer communication allows direct connections without depending on centralized intermediaries.

2. Distributed function abstractions using cryptographic protocols create and maintain shared, immutable, and verifiable records of transactions and events across all nodes used by a blockchain.

3. Decentralized autonomous applications are self-governing λ-calculus Namespace entities that operate according to self-defined rules as smart contracts with minimal human intervention and without physical dependencies.

4. Global applications run as distributed locally secure telecommunication, health, and education nodes using local administration authority.

Attacks that penetrate the superuser administrator cannot be patched. The superuser is a design feature of binary computers. When the nation is frozen as it was on July 19th, 2024, it is a costly disaster caused by human error with an international scale of damage. Disruptions extended to Australia, New Zealand, India, Japan, and the UK. In addition, 911 services failed, and outage monitors reported that critical services at Amazon Web Services, Instagram, eBay, Visa, and ADT halted, and these outages ripple through many others who depend on their services. Disruption continues and rebounds across cyberspace as a digital tsunami.

For days, U.S. airports were jammed with passengers unable to fly. American, Delta and United Airlines faced groundings due to communications failures caused by this single point of failure, amplified by the crude approach of software security as a flawed software update. Supermarkets, banks, telecommunications companies, and TV broadcasters were all affected. Like COVID-19, hospital outages and loss of emergency services no doubt cause life-saving failures.

According to media reports, international airports were also impacted by the communications failures that week, including:

1. Frankfurt Airport in Germany experienced delays and cancellations of hundreds of flights.

2. Dubai International Airport in the United Arab Emirates diverted flights to regional airports.

3. Toronto Pearson International Airport in Canada suffered from long queues, baggage handling, and disruptions in check-in services.

4. Hong Kong International Airport in China faced problems with its air traffic control system and passenger information displays.

5. Sydney Airport in Australia encountered issues with its online booking system and security screening.

Science is the only way to avoid such problems and run industrial society indefinitely, safely, and productively for future generations. Cyberspace is a global utility and a threat to everyone. How many synchronised attacks or single-point-of-failure outages are too many? It is an awkward question when land, sea, air, and space defence costs so much and when no expense is spared for the bridge failure in Baltimore or the COVID-19 pandemic. Given that scientific solutions exist, just one is too many, and it is irresponsible for industry and the government to think otherwise. It is a debilitating problem with an unacceptable end game, a social impact of lost trust in the national government, and a technology-driven downward spiral toward dictatorship. It must be resolved before it is too late. Trusted computer science must be the guaranteed foundation of 21st-century cyberspace.

Flawless machine code changes everything. It removes all the distracting baggage of centralization, all single points of failure, all undetected malware, and the road to dictatorship. At the same time, Capability-Limited-Object-Oriented-Machine-Code adds traceability, providence, and usage history, a fingerprint on every digital object in cyberspace. Providence is vital in detecting deepfakes, authoring signed documents, and guaranteeing democracy operates with the same standards and traditions established over centuries.

It is not an option. It is a necessity for the survival of civilization as opposed to Orwellian dictatorship. The flaws in binary computers must be removed as quickly and smoothly as possible. Computer insecurity impacts the progress of democratic society because it jeopardizes the trust, values, principles, enforcement, punishment, and other practices that keep democracy on the rails, as established by our founders.

The unacceptable present is undetected crimes, unpunished crooks, global conflicts, international malware, untraceable activity, and undetected hacks. Corruption destroys the foundations of this Constitutional Republic and gradually replaces America as the beacon of freedom with unelected digital dictatorships like China, Russia, Iran, and North Korea. The tragedy is underway, and it all stems from the unscientific chaos of the one-sided binary computer.

The right solution starts with the ideas of the mind, like theoretical mathematics, built as function abstractions translated into digital computations by the science of the λ-calculus, enforced by the type-limited digital boundaries of capability-limited addressing. Function abstractions have a long history of success that began in the physical world as the abacus. The Abacus employs the abstraction of the human hand, with many threaded hands as a private cellular array. Each rail is a decimal number and a computational cell bound to one function-tight, decimal data digit. The abstractions support three functions: addition, subtraction, and reset, but the cells only count from zero to nine, with an overflow or underflow possibility. It scales as an array of rails, and each rail represents another hand. It is a threaded chain of atomic abstractions of many human hands for more significant numbers that scale scientifically to infinity minus one.

This form of computational threads also supports individual privacy and security. The slide rule adds mathematical functionality without losing individuality, privacy, and security by embedding the algorithms as scales unexposed to human errors. A mathematical class encapsulating the computational machinery that can solve every mathematical function, it foretells the essence of the Church-Turing Thesis, which encapsulates the Turing Machine as the engine of the λ-calculus.

At the height of the Industrial Revolution, Charles Babbage went further. He designed and prototyped flawless mathematical machines, the Difference and the Analytical Engine. He abstracted the essential arithmetic functions with multiplication and division, and from this,

Ada Lovelace could solve the Bernoulli series as a complex function abstraction. None of the mechanical implementation details were exposed, allowing Ada to program Babbage's Thinking Machine mathematically, just as taught to children at school.

This history is the scientific story of computer science, and the family tree of computer science must inherit these ideas. The science of function abstractions leads to the Church- Turing Thesis and λ-calculus. It avoids the binary computer, virtual memory, branded operating system, and all the variations of branded baggage covered above.

The binary computer is a flawed shortcut, a dangerous cutoff proposed by John von Neumann after World War II when digital computers began. It worked for one edge condition, the stand-alone mainframe, provided it was locked in secure rooms and guarded by experts. For every other case, it is a dead-end canyon no different to the cutoffs the pioneers who ventured West took crossing their unknowns. They all led to death and destruction[29].

Likewise, the von Neumann binary cutoff created more problems than it solved. Unavoidably and inevitably, it lacks the science to save civilization from itself. The cutoff cannot copy Ada's achievement or what the Abacus, the slide rule, and Babbage's Thinking Machines achieved. Computer science is a mental process of named ideas as abstractions framed by the human mind. While Babbage dreamed of his flawless functional masterpiece, the Analytical Engine, the binary computers fail because they are physical and centralized instead of functional and distributed. Thus, everything stopped for the first Big Freeze on July 19th, 2024.

The growth of centralization, single points of failure, and digital dictators must end because the risks and consequences are too severe not to do so. Civilization is unnecessarily placed at risk. Next

---

29   The Hastings Cutoff added hardship, and starvation for the ill-fated Donner Party. The Lassen Cutoff involved steep, and rocky terrain, dense forests, and scarce water. Everything was lost, and some resorted to cannibalism. The Meek Cutoff became a treacherous slog without water or food.

time, supply chains could fail, and like the earlier misled pioneers, the hardships grow, and people die. Heaven forbid we resort to cannibalism. Binary computers can create global catastrophes because they are weapons of mass destruction, and the single points of failure cannot be patched. The superuser is the grim reaper of a digital doomsday. The WMD is more virile and extensive than an atomic bomb because it favours enemy dictatorships. It is already in the hands of America's unscrupulous enemy states led by Big Brother, motivated and digitally equipped to dominate the world.

Computers and cyberspace are the destiny and the destination of humanity, life, democracy, freedom, justice, and civilization worldwide. It must be perfected and respected to be trusted. As such, there is no room for lack of trust, undetected malware, single-point-of- failures, silly programming errors, or administration mistakes, accidental or deliberate. Only Mother Nature solves these problems; only science enforced by the golden tokens of λ- calculus, and the digital girders, and guard rails, the digital ironwork of capability-based computer science energized by Capability-Limited-Object-Oriented-Machine-Code, works.

In the summer of 1843, Ada Lovelace programmed the first twenty-five lines of documented code. As her letters show, she exchanged and refined her ideas daily with Charles Babbage. Quickly and cleanly, they understood each other and the machine code intellectually. Separated by time and space through the symbols of theoretical mathematics, these statements resonate today and forever. They used expressions of scientific truth taught in schoolrooms worldwide, something impossible with binary computers. Binary machine code is proprietary, unscientific gibberish, a branded, incomprehensible machine dialect that speaks in digital riddles.

There is no truth theorem to frame the workings of any binary computer. The centralized baggage of von Neumann's shortcut stranded his binary wagon without the wheels to progress and crisscross cyberspace. The centralization of functionality led to single points of failure depending on the operating systems, administrators, languages, off-line compilations, and other related baggage hidden by the un-patchable, un-trustable super- user. It is an unforgivable scientific scandal. All the effort of decades is lost in growing mounds of garbage plagued by malware rats. John von Neumann's cutoff is another dead- end canyon, a more deadly trap for citizens in cyberspace.

GENES AND THE FAMILY TREE

The family tree for computers as a science did not start with John von Neumann's cutoff, the binary computer. It started thousands of years ago at the beginning of civilization with the Abacus and the abstraction of a decimal number. It is the root example of atomic functional computation as a cellular secure thread for private computation codified in 1936 as the λ- calculus. The cells of computation inherit the mechanisms of a 'selfish gene' to borrow from Richard Dawkins[30], the eminent biologist's idea about biological life and evolution applied to cellular λ-calculus computations. This protected cellular framework hardens abstractions of the mind as secure atomic computations that inherit cookie-cutter boundaries of type-limited digital security. Each computational cell abstracts a functional thing one at a time as a set of specifically named functions. For the abacus, each cell is in a decimal number framed into an array as a more significant number that adds and subtracts.

The slide rule is another hardened atomic mechanism where algorithms are embossed as scales on sliding rods. The full range

---

30   Richard Dawkins' idea of the selfish gene is that evolution is driven by the survival, and atomic, and cellular replication of genes, not organisms, individuals, or groups. Dawkins argues that genes act selfishly to maximize the chances of being passed on to the next generation. This theory challenges the notion that natural selection operates for the good of the species but instead emphasizes the role of genetic variation, and competition among genes.

of theoretical mathematics no longer needs to be learned and remembered in an individual's head. However, it remains the same distributed thread as a secure private computation begun by the Abacus that culminated in the λ- calculus.

The Analytical Engine proposed further simplifications as a complete mathematical Namespace of function abstractions found today in every handheld calculator. Babbage began with the four arithmetic functions (+, -, x, and /) shown in row one of Table 5 Example Symbols Used in Theoretical Mathematics by Subject. All the remaining functions found in today's calculators are scientific derivatives of the four primary functions. Most importantly, Babbage supported abstract variables (a, b, c, and so on) that made his solution functionally far more potent than statically bound numeric variables in a binary computer.

As taught at school, arithmetic has four essential functions that deal with the initial number operations: addition, subtraction, multiplication, and division. Arithmetic also includes concepts like fractions, decimals, percentages, ratios, and how parts of a whole are represented when comparing different quantities. Arithmetic is the oldest form of mathematics, dating back to ancient civilizations. It is needed for everyday calculations, like counting, measuring, budgeting, and estimating. Arithmetic is also the foundation for every one of the more advanced branches of mathematics, as shown in Table 5 Example Symbols Used in Theoretical Mathematics by Subject.

For example, trigonometry deals with the relationships between the sides, angles of triangles, functions, and identities derived from them. Trigonometry is an extension of arithmetic, using addition, subtraction, multiplication, division, powers, and roots to calculate triangles' lengths, areas, and angles. Trigonometry introduces new concepts, such as trigonometric ratios, inverse trigonometric functions, and trigonometric identities, which help solve equations and model periodic phenomena. Trigonometry has applications in many fields, including astronomy, navigation at sea, engineering machines, and understanding physics and geometry.

In every case, each function has a symbol to abstract the idea into a unique notion. The symbol represents the function as an immutable token, symbolising the meaning of the function as an abstraction and securing the details. Moreover, as Ada wrote in her notes in 1843, she recognized that the symbols for music are abstractions of sounds and notes, the text of literature abstracts speech, and art is likewise an abstraction of vision. Indeed, anything the human mind can conceive is an abstraction that can be shared in a word once an immutable symbol is agreed upon.

Abstractions are the foundation mechanisms of the Abacus, the slide rule, mechanical and digital computers, programs, and the computer science theory expressed by the λ-calculus. Encapsulating Turing's atomic computer hides the vulnerable implementation details within each abstraction's scope and perimeter. The result is that the λ-calculus oversees every computation as a distributed private thread, just like the Abacus and the slide rule.

Digital abstraction is a computational technique that allows the λ-calculus to manipulate symbols and expressions representing data, operations, and things of any size, complexity, physical location, or geographic structure. Digital abstraction helps design and implement efficient algorithms, protocols, and connected ideas that can perform tasks that are too difficult or impossible for humans without a reliable tool.

For example, the global communications network is built from equipment, sometimes over one hundred years old, from many equipment suppliers built to the standards of different nations. The digital twin of this global physical system, equipment, and functions can be abstracted according to ideas. One such idea is how it is used, and another is how it is constructed internationally, nationally, regionally, all the way down to the physical endpoints. Mobile networks introduce another level of abstraction related to carrier networks that allow roaming tethered to carrier services and customer-chosen plans.

Overlaid on this are questions like the use of encryption to secure communications. The centralization characteristics of the binary computer only complicate the construction of a digital twin by imposing additional orthogonal constraints that have nothing to do with the motivating task. The λ-calculus simplifies everything by a process of reduction.

Reduction simplifies the mathematical model of computation using functions as the basic units of computation. The reduction applies rules that replace parts of an expression with simpler or equivalent parts until no more reductions are possible. The goal is to reach a form that no rule can further reduce. The standard rules of reduction are:

1. Alpha reduction changes the name of a bound variable (a variable that is an argument of a function) to avoid name collisions. For example, λx.x can be 'alpha-reduced' to λy.y since both functions have the same meaning.

2. Beta reduction applies a function to its argument by substituting the argument for the bound variable in the function body. For example, (λx.x + 1)(2) can be beta-reduced to 2 + 1 by replacing x with 2 in the function body.

3. Eta reduction eliminates unnecessary abstraction by removing a function that does nothing but apply another function to its argument. For example, λx.(f x) can be eta-reduced to f since both functions have the same effect on any argument.

Point-to-point communication control is the practical result of this reduction, and the consequence is encryption as an endpoint concern rather than a carrier concern. Only the programmer of the encryption abstraction needs to understand the mathematical rules of encryption. A simple interface allows encrypting and decrypting messages using a golden token to unlock the required function.

Similarly, the power of artificial intelligence to perform tasks like facial recognition, natural language processing, or game playing is directly accessible through symbols. These symbols map directly into Capability-Limited-Object-Oriented-Machine-Code, removing the complexity of spaghetti code by removing all the physical to logical complexity of binary computers at every level of abstraction.

Binary machine code is the root cause that cannot be overcome in this first-generation version of cyberspace. The abstractions cannot be networked because they are trapped by a stand-alone compilation inherited from the mainframe age of the Cold War. The binary network cannot achieve the power of reduction because it cannot access abstraction without all the redundant baggage created when the mainframe age began in the 1950s and 1960s.

Capability-Limited-Object-Oriented-Machine-Code bypasses all this baggage by returning to the science of 1936, where everything is simplified and concentrated as high-level application-oriented statements that allow efficient machine code statements that improve with every innovation as a worldwide capability.

Capability-Limited-Object-Oriented-Machine-Code democratizes computer science internationally, equally, securely, and privately as individual threads. Every critical advance in high-cost areas, like blockchains, artificial intelligence, cryptography, financial modelling, game theory, and other expensive services, are all simplified by symbolic computation and integrated directly into individual threads of computation, bypassing all of the dangerous and incompetent baggage needed by the illogical physical commands of the binary computer.

On the list of advantages and benefits of Capability-Limited-Object-Oriented-Machine- Code is future-safe evolution. The λ-calculus is the bridge to the everlasting future because, as science, it is everlasting and, like Ada's Bernoulli code, remains future-safe and fail-safe. Free from technology implementation details, machine code that lasts forever, like Ada's Bernoulli code, of readable mathematics. The expression of abstractions in an application-oriented namespace.

Capability-Limited-Object-Oriented-Machine-Code includes secure golden tokens, structured digital ironwork to protect and secure each symbolic name, and its implementation details in cyberspace. As outlined in Table 11, Listed Advantages of Capability-Limited Object-Oriented Machine Code, complexity is simplified by symbolic machine code. At the same time, individual privacy and information security are guaranteed using the power of λ-calculus.

Complex abstractions can directly and securely assess access to critical functionality with global reach without the dangerous and unnecessary physical overheads associated with the centralized baggage of operating systems and compilers, resulting in networked fragmentation.

Table 11, Listed Advantages of Capability-Limited Object-Oriented Machine Code

Subject Areas	Digital Ironwork - Advantages of using CLOOMC
Church-Turing Thesis	Computer computations encapsulated atomically by the laws of λ-calculus and the boundaries of capability-limited addressing.
Physical to logical mapping	The cookie-cutter solution of λ-calculusis implemented once as a foundation machine technology to benefit every line of code in cyberspace.
Capability-Limited Addressing	Every object is named and protected by digital boundaries as safely typed, data-tight, and function-tight information.
Immutable Symbolic Tokens	Immutable digital tokens reference digital objects as named information distinct from mutable binary data.
Digital Type Separation	Engineered separation of binary instruction activity from Church Instruction actions that guarantee capability tokens are immutable and recognized as different from binary data
Type Preservation	Every digital object is type protected as a machine type (data or token) or an abstract type (function limitations of an abstraction).
Namespace Preservation	A Namespace is a distinct digital object that lists and maps symbolic names as immutable digital tokens to the object as a digital implementation in cyberspace.
Class of Function	Names class of functions secured dynamically as a subroutine call in a computational thread.

Thread of Computation	A hybrid abstraction defining the thread by the machine registers and suspension conditions of a stack of class computational steps in last-in-first-out order
Executable Function Abstractions	Named machine code Church-Instructions call named abstractions of any complexity as symbolic (readable) program steps in a global computation.
Telecommunications (per Supplier)	Global reach from a simple distributed software architecture located anywhere
Cryptography	Design analysis for secure private threads throughout networked cyberspace
Automation (One per subject)	Fail-safe machine commands composed of comprehensible names of immutable namespace tokens
Artificial Intelligence (Per LLM & Subject Matter)	Enhanced algorithms and functions accessible to individual threads of secure, private computations in machine code
Blockchains	Direct and secure access to critical fail-safe software functionality with global reach and without unnecessary centralized binary overheads
Financial Modelling	Analyse complex financial data to make informed decisions on a Namespace basis for individual businesses, international organizations, and nations.
Game Theory	Enhanced problem-solving skills to drive local, machine-level innovation
Theoretical Mathematics	Exploration of complex mathematical concepts and proving intricate theorems for individuals, schools, and universities worldwide
Independent Nations (one per Nation)	Local formulation of government laws for democracy under national control without outside interference
International Agreements (one be standard)	Direct access to global agreements as international function abstractions, for example, the United Nations.
Education	Easy access for schools and universities to the latest research and training offered internationally

Other Namespaces	Cyberspace grows by adding software such as Namespace Applications rather than physical servers that are hard to access, secure, and share using binary computers.

For example, the abstraction of global telecommunication exemplified in Equation 1 introduced earlier is a fail-safe machine command composed using the comprehensible names of the immutable-namespace-tokens that understand but hide the functional complexity of the global telecommunication application.

From left to right, the first token is *myConnection*. The token is the returned variable created incrementally as the thread computes the request. It is a dynamic structure built as the individual function abstractions perform their private tasks. The tokens can be taken from pools of free tokens engineered in advance or created from templates on the fly. When the result returns, the call is connected. The returned function abstraction is a digital twin of the equipment used to build the call, potentially a global connection.

The initial request is serviced by a protected call to a function abstraction called *Switch.* using the fail-safe Church Instruction named 'CALL.' The called abstraction is defined by this second token *Switch.* This token offers the switch functions in a nodal function-tight list that catalogues accessible functionality as a function-tight list. The example uses the

Connect function, which takes two variables specifying the two endpoints; the origin (the caller) is named *me*, and the far end defines the abstraction of *myMother*.

This statement does not identify the telephone handset as the best endpoint; perhaps a cell phone, a landline, a PC, or even her status requesting a text message to be sent. All these details are unknown, hidden, and resolved by the thread, allowing parallel actions that locally or remotely resolve each question at the right time. Events clarify local conditions when optimum decisions are made with the minimum complexity.

Each name in these expressions is an immutable, golden token, a capability-limited pointer to the named abstraction. The golden

tokens have specific access rights enumerated and embellished like the jewels in a sword of state or slogans on a chain of office. They enumerate the power assigned to the referenced role of the object in focus. It is a digital key to unlock access rights to the digital details in approved ways. Unlocking access to the specifically named digital implementation referenced by Capability-Limited-Object-

Oriented-Machine-Code allows the program to unfold complexity like a flower in the sunshine.

So, returning to the example in Equation 1, there is a hierarchy of named tokens hanging from each abstraction that provides type limited access to the precise methods needed to complete the program, such as a telephone call. At every step, the Capability Limited- Object-Oriented-Machine-Code identifies the next function abstraction as a global location with any attached equipment th location might access.

It means a crucial productivity difference exists, not just because a the centralized binary baggage is removed, and distribution include security at every step, but because the golden tokens of the λ-calculi add the power and productivity of functional programming. Fo example, the centralized risk of the confused deputy attack removed. Transferring control to the operating system to acce a hardware device is replaced by an in-line call to a device driv function abstraction with the appropriate golden token to acce the device hardware as an approved authority with correctly type access rights.

Individual computational thread controls these compl computations that start with an 'off-hook' request from a speci device, an abstraction for a handset, that indeed could be an ima on a computer screen. The thread receives this golden token t the specific endpoint, in this example, *me*. The thread uses t abstraction to collect the destination to call from the endpo abstraction by voice or keys as locally defined. It might be diall numbers, keyed in or spoken depending on the options availal

for device abstraction, preference setting, and device activity. For example, when the next event is 'on-hook,' the call ends, and any dynamic objects are released, the thread ends and can take on another task.

The abstractions are nodes in the Telecommunication Namespace hierarchy that express the DNA of the local application. DNA shapes the software as a dynamic design, the instances of the namespace as a digital species. This DNA structures events as a control system orthogonal to the inheritance hierarchy of the family tree. For telecommunications, the DNA spans the world. This DNA structure defines a behavioural blueprint of the species that resolves the rules of international and national variations, one abstraction at a time.

So, when I call *mySisterMary,* who lives in Freetown, Sierra Leone, West Africa, the connection is routed to her endpoint using intermediate connections dictated by present conditions. None of these essential details complicates the simplicity of the initial request. The details are resolved individually through local abstraction chosen as the call setup proceeds. If the call uses a landline, an undersea cable, a satellite, or the internet, it matters not, providing call requirements are met by the abstractions invoked by the DNA of the Namespace.

A different example is cryptography, the art of secret writing and private communication. Capability-Limited-Object-Oriented-Machine-Code offers options to program control encrypted security links that remain private and protect personal information from prying eyes. In a binary computer, nothing is private. The operating system dictates and observes everything. Democracy demands the opposite alternatives only found by using Capability- Limited-Object-Oriented-Machine-Code.

The advantages of expressing complex word symbols in machine code go well beyond cryptography. Marrying machine code with complex applications like cryptography paves the way for secured point-to-point communication channels. Privacy is essential for freedom and secret votes in a democratic society—likewise, secure payment systems and digital signatures connect everyday services dynamically across the interactive world.

Importantly, Capability-Limited-Object-Oriented-Machine-Code means faster algorithms with richer functions used by individual computation threads that anyone can learn to code. By leveraging symbolic computation, computer science ensures confidentiality, integrity, innovation, and authenticity of data and information exchanged as intelligent systems. The intersection of symbolic computing and artificial intelligence is the key to building autonomous systems that securely communicate and collaborate worldwide, applying local standards as needed in every case, as demonstrated by the telecommunications example developed for PP250.

In theoretical mathematics, symbolic computing opens avenues for network exploration of mathematical foundations to help research in every branch of science. Using Capability- Limited-Object-Oriented-Machine-Code, computers analyse complex algorithms, design new schemes, strengthen security worldwide as a secure and powerful tool to push the boundaries of scientific knowledge, and democratically enhance problem-solving skills for every individual worldwide.

Every application is empowered to include AI, financial modelling, game theory, and other niche areas that require secure global communication and symbolic computing. Abstracting applications through symbolic computing enhances networked functionality. It resolves cyber threats, protects valuable digital assets from malicious actors, and unlocks a new world of possibilities, all secured in depth and detail by default and under program control.

Incorporating Capability-Limited-Object-Oriented-Machine-Code leads to breakthroughs and advancements that reshape the future of technology, science, automation, humanity, civilization, and democracy while avoiding crime and dictatorship. Embracing the power of a second generation of computer science can unleash the full potential of cyber society as a visionary solution in the digital age.

Capability-Limited-Object-Oriented-Machine-Code revolutionizes programming and the approach to problem-solving. Harnessing the power of symbols in machine code creates the technology of artificial intelligence and neural networks to tackle complex problems with ease and precision. It opens possibilities beyond the boundaries of what is possible in every field. The essential advantage is the ability to share ideas quickly as symbols. Binary computers cannot share ideas; they can only share data as a binary value.

Symbols are a complex hierarchy, the digital DNA of a programmed application as a species. The DNA allows the versioning and evolution of the underlying structure of problems to identify patterns and develop elegant digital multi-dimensional implementations, which are not apparent when working with procedural binary programs trapped within a compiled binary image. It streamlines problem-solving to arrive at better, secure, efficient, and practical solutions.

Capability-Limited-Object-Oriented-Machine-Code is crucial when reasoning about complexity. It speeds up estimates and optimises decision-making. The ability to link Capability-Limited-Object-Oriented-Machine-Code with network services as function abstractions enhances code intelligence, performance, and results, improving results and understanding for every application.

In every realm, it allows the direct, intimate use of remote systems functionally and confidently to identify vulnerabilities, strengthen security, and stay ahead of cyber threats. It has become increasingly important as data privacy and cybersecurity are top priorities for organizations worldwide.

In conclusion, Capability-Limited-Object-Oriented-Machine-Code advances every field of computer science. The innovative technology harnesses science to its full potential, democratically for everyone, because it steps beyond the limitations of World War II and decades of centralized mainframes to enhance problem-solving by reshaping computer science around network function abstractions and the universal process of human thought. Individual citizens benefit internationally, even pushing dictatorial nations to offer democratic freedom, equality, and individual justice. Adopting Capability-Limited-Object-Oriented-Machine-Code is the critical change for a world run by Cyberspace where the dangers are digital, but the possibilities are endless.

DIGITAL TWINS

A digital twin represents an idea, a physical object, or a system in the virtual world of universal cyberspace. A twin can control, automate, simulate, and predict the past, present, and future. The idea originated using binary computers in the aerospace industry, where engineers used them to test and improve aircraft and spacecraft design. The PP250 created digital twins for the global telecommunication network. Digital twins are significant in other domains, including manufacturing, healthcare, energy, and transportation. These Digital Twins enhance details, efficiency, quality, testing, and innovation. In the future, Capability- Limited-Object-Oriented-Machine-Code, in conjunction with digital twins, enables immersive and interactive experiences in virtual or augmented reality through holograms that, like the λ-calculus, bridge the gap between the intellectual, the physical, and the digital worlds.

In the interconnected digital world, symbolic addressing is vital to express and share ideas that can only be exchanged cleanly as symbols that do far more than provide a static representation. With Capability-Limited-Object-Oriented-Machine-Code, the symbol can be entered, and the complexity can be experienced functionally. It is the whole meaning of the Enter access right invented for PP250.

To elaborate on the future of the digital twin, consider Dr Who, a BBC TV character who flew the spaceship TARDIS, standing for Time and Relative Dimension In Space. This device travels through time and space, changing its appearance to blend in with the environment.

It is more extensive inside than outside and has multiple rooms and corridors to accommodate the passengers' various needs and preferences. The TARDIS is controlled by a console that connects to the ship's subconscious matrix, which allows users to navigate temporal and spatial dimensions. It also has a personality and a will, sometimes taking the Doctor and his companions to unexpected places and times. The TARDIS is an idea about the most advanced and mysterious future technology. It is a source of wonder and adventure for Dr Who and his friends, and as a Digital Twin, it may one day exist as realized virtuality.

A Digital Twin is realized virtuality represented by complex function abstractions. Implementing a Digital Twin makes the ideal clear as a virtualization and cyberspace's past, present, and future. It is increasingly important as software expands to represent cyber society in every conceivable way, including the most precious ideas of individuality, family, nationality, democracy, and civilization. Capability-Limited-Object-Oriented-Machine- Code enhances, democratizes, and accelerates this progress. It allows for manipulating a shared idea scientifically using mathematics, expressions, proposals, and life forms, defining the twin as a functional, accurate, digital representation of λ-calculus abstractions. It is the only efficient way to share complex ideas digitally and symbolically through secure digital virtualization in Cyberspace. Professionals in any field who directly understand their subject can model it in cyberspace utilizing named ideas in Capability-Limited-Object- Oriented-Machine-Code. By simplifying computer science, we enhance problem-solving and empower individual skills to improve overall decision-making, especially regarding global activities like politics, education, and medicine.

Table 12 The Advantages of Capability-Limited-Object-Oriented-Machine-Code for Individuals

Topic	Importance
Namespace Computing	Arrange structured and secure interaction of the subject matter as symbolic expressions and equations, enabling accurate and efficient complex data analysis.

| Risk and Namespace Management | Object-oriented machine code allows for symbolic manipulation of abstraction as a single capability. It is a powerful tool for incremental and safely distributed mitigation of risks in every application. |
| Predictive Modelling | Allows for analysis of data to make informed decisions about the future by uncovering patterns and trends. |

One crucial area is financial modelling. Using Capability-Limited-Object-Oriented-Machine- Code computations, create digital twins as models that accurately and directly reflect the complexities of individual financial markets. These models improve predictions, reduce risk, and optimize investments because the models can share and distinguish functionality far more sophisticated and nuanced than traditional binary computers can achieve. It always leads to well-informed decision-making and better outcomes by harnessing the power to create robust methods resistant to attacks and breaches, safeguarding the integrity of financial transactions and information.

In addition to financial modelling and cryptography, symbolic computing plays a crucial role in other areas of finance, such as game theory and artificial intelligence. By applying symbolic computation techniques to these fields, computer professionals can gain deeper insights into complex decision-making processes and develop more sophisticated algorithms for optimizing outcomes by combining several high-cost applications as successive statements in Capability-Limited-Object-Oriented-Machine-Code. Adding artificial intelligence, for example, enhances the capabilities of expert financial traders to create problem-solving algorithms, leading to more profitable trades and better risk management strategies for their family, friends, and clients.

Overall, the importance of Capability-Limited-Object-Oriented-Machine-Code cannot be overstated. From individuals with unique skills in niche areas to one day the first quantum computers, interworking with artificial intelligence, cryptography, theoretical mathematics, financial modelling, and game theory, mastering the principles of symbolic computation is essential to stay ahead in a rapidly evolving and competitive world. By embracing symbolic computing and harnessing its power, the nation unlocks new possibilities, undreamed of innovation, with simplified problem-solving that leads to prosperity in a dynamic, changing, digitally secure world.

THE END GAME

This trilogy lays out the technical arguments for computer science to adopt Capability- Limited-Object-Oriented-Machine-Code. They are overwhelming. The scientific solution solves all the corruption problems in cyberspace, from malware to the Big Freeze, while dramatically improving productivity and deskilling and democratizing the platform of cybersociety for the eternal future. Outdated, first-generation binary computers cause these troublesome problems. Computers must empower society, not frighten them. Computers must apply science, not flawed shortcuts that lead to catastrophe. To ignore the flawless history of computers that began with the Abacus and democratized progress is a grand tragedy that damages the progress of civilization.

Capability-Limited-Object-Oriented-Machine-Code restores functional science to computer science. The natural advantages of a Church-Turing Machine following the rules of the λ-calculus could and would competitively replace the binary computer and secure the future, but the digital dictators are afraid to take the risk. The costs and risks are beyond their interest in the global marketplace. If dictatorship wins over democracy, they also win because that is what they sell.

China is no democracy and may never be. It remains a vast market for binary computers, as do Russia, Iran, and other dictatorships that use secret police and authoritarian surveillance. These surveillance states are not our friends in cyberspace. They are antithetically opposed to our democratic ways, and we are at war in cyberspace. It is a war we are losing because of the binary computer and the unwillingness of industry to risk changing direction.

The established industry looks at the problem, assessing the need to change from their business perspective, and resoundingly, the investment risks to their global business are too high. From a purely business perspective, they are happy to see international dictatorships run the world. The choice is not their business. It is the citizens' choice. Selling dictatorships is easier and improves revenue without regard for national differences.

So, the threats remain for democracy to decide. Will the frequency and breadth of malware and the Big Freeze crash the economy, or is dictatorship and increased authoritarian oppression too much to take? It is a version of Abraham Lincoln's question addressed at Gettysburg. He spoke at the site of one of the bloodiest battles of the American Civil War, which was fought between the Union and the Confederate states over the issues of slavery and secession.

However, in his speech on November 19, 1863, at a national cemetery in Gettysburg, Pennsylvania, Abraham Lincoln, then president of the United States, reaffirmed the principles of equality and democracy that inspired the founding of the United States. Lincoln declared that the war tested whether such a nation could endure. He also honoured the soldiers who sacrificed their lives for the cause of preserving the Union and securing freedom for the enslaved. He concluded by urging the living to continue the unfinished work of the dead and to ensure that the government of the people, by the people, for the people, shall not perish from the earth.

The Gettysburg Address is one of American history's most influential and memorable speeches carved onto the Lincoln Memorial on the banks of the Potomac in Washington, D.C.[31] It is also one of the shortest, lasting only about two minutes and containing 272 words. It has been quoted and referenced by many leaders,

---

31   Lincoln Memorial - Wikipedia

writers, and activists to invoke its immortal ideals of democracy and human rights, and again, as ever, Americans are faced with defending this ideal: will the nation endure living with enemies so close at hand in undefended cyberspace?

What is certain is that cyberspace has changed everything and continues to do so, and the shortcut von Neumann chose in 1945 was wrong. A national Donner party now freezes in cyberspace and is unable to survive World War III, a global war in Cyberspace with the enemies of democracy. Using binary computers is as dangerous and incapable as using the wooden wagons of earlier pioneers under worst-case conditions.

These problems began with one mistake in 1945, when John von Neumann chose the dangerous binary cutoff. The only option if the Lincoln Memorial means anything is to change direction. We, the people, should make this choice by voting with our pocketbooks, but we have no choice because real competition is suppressed by suppliers who sustain backward compatibility. Only inspired investments can fix this; because the national risk is existential, several options should be implemented in parallel following an updated COVID-19 plan that includes the free distribution of the vaccine, this time a Church-Turing machine.

The soft spot in binary computers is the superuser architecture created to hide virtual memory hardware and the dictatorial services of the operating system. This single point of failure became the cause of ransomware and the foundation stone of centralized digital dictatorship. When malware penetrates a superuser, all bets are off, and to stop malware, vendors increase authoritarian controls—a vicious cycle leading downhill to unprecedented, unavoidable industrial and national disasters.

This vicious cycle cannot be reversed or adjusted as a hybrid alternative, and the end game is unacceptable to the spirit of a nation of citizens founded on equality and freedom. The downhill cycle is repetitively demonstrated in the most extreme case by ransomware, malicious software encrypting the victim's data, and demanding a ransom for the decryption key—now amplified by AI as a synchronized Big Freeze when the economy shudders to a halt.

The downhill cycle threatens individuals, businesses, and government agencies. It can halt all networked services after penetrating any administrator account. The single point of failure culminates in a Big Freeze when every computer network-wide stops, as established by the CrowdStrike Holdings, Inc. catastrophe[32]. The next round of attacks exploiting this fatal weakness stops the industrial world in its tracks.

Ransomware demonstrates the power of corruption in binary cyberspace. It all began with hacking. The digital foundations of the binary computer are fatally flawed. From there, the superuser and the network connections are single points of failure, and, when penetrated, lead to ransomware today and another Big Freeze tomorrow. Even lesser malware problems rob society of growth and progress. Malware is the rotten case that ruins the apple barrel.

However, another significant problem looms over binary cyber society. The binary computer is founded as the purveyor of centralized surveillance and authoritarianism—the enforcer as the henchmen of digital dictatorship. When built from binary computers, cyberspace takes away whatever it offers with the other hand. Cyberspace is addictive because it offers many fascinating advantages while hiding one overwhelming threat of digital dictatorship.

Dictatorship is the ultimate end game if binary computers run cyberspace. The system hides corruption and malware, which leads to increased surveillance and suppression. A downhill cycle unavoidably leads to an Orwellian hell. Centralization, surveillance, authoritarian henchmen, and centralized dictatorship are unacceptable, either in the natural world or in cyberspace.

There are reasons why dictatorships fail. It begins and ends with centralization. Oppression limits freedom and promotes naked fear organized by secret service and palace guards intended to prevent the dictator's overthrow. Fear alienates and antagonizes the citizens.

---

32   On 19 July 2024, American cybersecurity company CrowdStrike distributed a faulty update to its Falcon Sensor security software that caused widespread problems with Microsoft Windows computers running as superuser software. As a result, 8.5 million systems crashed, and were unable to properly restart in what has been called the largest outage in the history of information technology, and "historic in scale".

Suppressing dissent violates human rights while monopolizing power provokes resistance and rebellion. Individuals seek freedom and justice. Some recent examples of dictators overthrown by popular uprisings include Nicolae Ceausescu of Romania, Muammar Gaddafi of Libya, and Hosni Mubarak in Egypt.

Dictatorships fail due to citizen unrest, as exemplified by the Soviet Union (the USSR). The state became a dictatorship ever since the Russian Revolution of 1917 when the Bolsheviks established a socialist state, followed by civil war. So, the Bolsheviks established a secret police, known as Cheka, to carry out mass executions against any opposition. Joseph Stalin rose to power and ruled as a dictator until he died in 1953. His reign was marked by terror, with brutal policies that resulted in the deaths of millions of Soviet citizens.

A highly centralized government organisation means that decision-making is concentrated, and the operating systems in cyberspace become the government's henchman. Rules are made by digital decree, enforced from above without any local considerations or of the founder's wishes and the laws of the land. A small elite group of unelected designers make every decision. The operating systems become the Cheka of a Soviet model of the dictatorship of the proletariat, which in practice means absolute control over the operations of the binary computer. It is a Marxist-Communist approach that employs the terror of ransomware to detect malware attacks that only increase authoritarianism. However, every attempt to detect the latest zero-day attack further suppresses individual citizens' freedom and independence.

Consider the dissolution of the Soviet Union in 1991, which stemmed from a combination of economic and political stagnation coupled with a crisis of confidence due to inefficiencies that stifled innovation. These same problems exist with the digital dictatorship of computer science. Centralized operating systems are fraught with misjudgement, mismanagement, malware corruption, and disproportionate attention on defending the indefensible. They cannot cope with local conditions, customs, cultures, and national democratic requirements because centralized digital dictators run everything. The stagnation grows from lacking competition, stifling all needed reforms and disconnecting the centralized core from their clients' expecting service. Any attempted reforms weaken the hold, increasing demands for independence and creating unacceptable chaos.

Competition is vital for cyber society and computer science to progress harmoniously, and the competition must be radical. The hybrid approach taken by the CRASH program allowed ideas to be stifled, and the prohibitive cost of semiconductor technology blocks radical competition. The Federal Government is mandated to overcome international threats and defend the nation. It must vaccinate us against our international enemies in cyberspace to preserve the government by and for the people.

Failure to create radical competition only continues chaos in cyberspace and the digital dictator's end game. The binary computer is the wrong path, the dangerous path of unacceptable risks and losing the American dream. Binary computers threaten American freedom. Enemies around the world use international cyberspace to attack the homeland. It is a war in cyberspace and a question of national defence.

Enemies can attack the heavily and increasingly computerized infrastructure. The freshwater pumps, the power grid, first responders, and especially cyberspace, by launching targeted ransomware attacks that take over control. Attacking cyberspace is a force multiplier, like a Big Freeze, when everything stops. The unforgeable tokens of authority as capability-limited keys to unlock authorized but limited privileges hardened by machine code is the only acceptable solution for computers as a functioning science following the Church-Turing Thesis, and it is needed soon.

An investment of $300 million to create a silicon Church-Turing computer following the PP250 example using all the latest technology advantages as competition to the binary computer is the vital step it takes to begin the change in direction. Other things can be approved later. It should be led as it was for the COVID-19 emergency with an industrial government plan for national vaccines, alternatives from significant suppliers that follow the Church-Turing Thesis, and apply Capability-Limited-Object-Oriented-Machine-Code, and explicitly remove any form of hardware priveledges or a central operating system. Given the government's ultimate responsibility to defend the Homeland as a nation, it is a trivial but vital investment for the Federal Government.

This low-cost, easily used, fail-safe, democratically distributed competition kills cyber threats. It wins World War III because the solution cannot be compromised, and private data cannot be accessed or encrypted when others cannot access a secret capability token. It applies object-oriented designs to isolate and encapsulate individual software components, making monitoring and controlling their interactions a local concern that can consider local customs and laws and removes all forms of single points of failure.

Capability-Limited-Object-Oriented-Machine-Code achieves all this and detects all malware and ransomware attacks in advance. Using symbolic tokens simplifies complexity and reduces code to a minimum but with far more power than binary procedures. Symbols enable advanced analysis and reasoning about the code and data to verify its integrity, trace its origin, and find inconsistencies. It also identifies, detects, and removes malicious code and data injected or from ransomware and malware attacks. Furthermore, using machine code, the most potent programming level that defines and executes instructions on the surface of computer science, the system performs the code directly without any intermediate layers of complexity and interpretation corrupted or exploited by accident or design.

To conclude, Capability-Limited-Object-Oriented-Machine-Code is the robust, efficient, and radical solution to the problems of binary cyberspace and protecting the USA from global enemies and deep state resistance. It achieves security benefits by combining science with capabilities, object orientation, and symbolic computations as dependable, trusted machine code. It democratically, securely, and reliably enhances cybersociety and protects the ideals of the USA with guaranteed engineered performance to enable another generation of possibilities for innovation and problem-solving.

APPENDIX A – ICCC 76

A Comprehensive System for Online Implementation of Privacy and Security Measures

T his Appendix is the oral presentation by K. J. Hamer-Hodges Plessey Telecom Research, U.K., at the Third International Conference on Computer Communications, Toronto, Canada, 3rd to 6th August 1976.

Abstract: Analogies are drawn between the demands of security-conscious computer communication systems and the natural solutions for privacy and security. The dependence upon hardware to mechanise bank safe deposit boxes is reviewed with historical examples of implementations founded on shared principles, highlighting the implementation of secure capability based computers.

Thank you, Mr. Chairman; - Good afternoon, everyone. When I told my wife about this the last time slot, my wife said, 'You realise you are the only thing preventing the audience from attending the banquet. '

As the only engineer on this expert legal panel, being the odd one out is doubly challenging. Nevertheless, I hope to build a bridge between our disciplines in our search for universal standards. By this, I mean traditional, socially acceptable, transparent data privacy and information security techniques. It is the case that engineers, as members of society, hold views on society's needs and satisfaction that correspond to any other significant section of the community. As such, engineers reflect a valid set of representative views.

But is the reverse true? Can the lay community, including lawyers and legislators, have an accurate view of my world of engineering and the inner world of computers and communications for us this afternoon? As the conference president said in his keynote speech yesterday, I believe this is hard; therefore, engineers have increased responsibility to resolve this challenging issue. It is the responsibility of the engineering community to forge this bridgehead, which is why, as the odd one out, I am here today.

Slide 1.

As I see things, I aim to share the vision of a bridgehead to build digital privacy and information security in digital computers and communications. My view is formed from two distinct influences: first, engineering - my training and experience, and second, my view of society - its need for satisfaction.

I build my bridgehead on fundamental observations concerning more widely implemented and quickly understood privacy and security traditions that began with civilisation's birth. It should prompt, even aggravate, further discussions, and I hope not just this afternoon.

I suggest two universal principles exist in all successful solutions: physical strength and logical integrity. Because of their recurring selection, these principles must be socially necessary, practical, and expected. Therefore, despite any legal vacuum, engineers have a recognised standard for developing systems that parallel natural or traditional approaches to control privacy and security, thereby preventing the dark side of humanity from winning.

I stand back at our chairman's request to discuss these issues without technical jargon. The intent of our session will, I hope, permit me to speak across and away from the details of my paper, providing a layman's overview of the technical subject matter.

Any alternative to a natural solution must be contrived. Contrived security is proprietary and opaque by nature. For example, the so-called General-Purpose Computer demands complex 'best practices.' Such skills are challenging to understand, impossible to sustain on a broad basis, and challenging for civilians to follow. Consequently, citizens do not recognise the external actions with critical internal needs. Most seriously, a contrived solution is exposed to inside and outside corruption and is in constant danger from anyone or anything with specialised knowledge and power. Thus, these systems can be hacked because disjointed but privileged modes of use weaken the implementation.

Even if we identify the social standards, how should we apply them? Yesterday, we heard about the Infonet system, which reflects the rules I want to discuss. However, the thoughtful ideas expressed by their work must be implemented at the most detailed level of digital activity; otherwise, the sale or purchase of a single password allows for the widespread invasion of privacy to occur internally, where a security vacuum exists.

Therefore, the standards must apply to every digital action throughout the computer, and this begins at the hardware level with the machine code that is the guts of the software and hardware system. Only when each instruction is fail-safe can everything else be protected, not just from each other but critically from the system itself. In such systems, the inner world mirrors the outside world, where all men are islands. The knowledge of a passcode provides no more than the seller already knows; like the Pyramids, a break-in does not provide automatic access to every internal chamber.

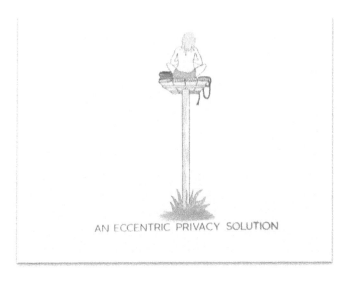

AN ECCENTRIC PRIVACY SOLUTION

Slide 2.

I now summarise four judgments concerning the standards created by natural selection. It is a reflective look at the implementation of capability-based computers that build on the mechanism of indirect, 'capability-limited' addressing, using the name of modular abstractions, instead of direct physical addressing to dangerously shared, monolithic storage.

This capability-limited approach atomically protects each digital chamber of a computer. Importantly, this indirection regulates the access rights to individual digital objects stored anywhere in local or networked memory. Using symbolic addressing hides the programmed objects as abstractions hidden by their unique name, represented by an immutable digital capability key. The immutable capability keys define the location and the access rights to the named digital resource.

Hence, managing programs, data, devices, and networks, whatever their digital form, is abstracted by the need to know a name and a least-privileged access mode. Capability lists define a universal method of secure modularity implemented by immutable private lists of keys. Keys are owned and hidden privately in a private hierarchical tree of keyrings. Individual objects are private and secure computational functions, data, classes, and namespace domains.

Capability-based computers deserve increased attention because the power to abstract and simultaneously secure each digital resource is fundamental to science, life, and mathematics. This ability is unique to capability-based computers. Abstractions bind, thereby hiding all details spanning all forms and hazards. Local and remote attacks and hardware failure detection are resolved at once.

Critically, capability-limited-addressing provides information security and data privacy at the lowest implementation level. Corruption cannot bypass these hardware checks, which are mathematically validated step by step for each machine instruction. It protects access rights to individual locations, as in a Bank's strongroom, at the atomic scale of individual memory location combined with customised access rights.

As a computer designer, I must explain what privacy and security mean to me. First, privacy is required to lock something important safely in memory, which is limited by controlled individual access rights. In contrast, security expresses the ability to lock others without a right to know out of private memory. In the simplest terms, privacy limits reading from locations in computer memory. In contrast, security limits writing to computer memory.

Slide 3.

Additional access modes limit running programs and unnecessary access to other modular function abstractions. Access rules are the prime object of my work in Telecommunications, where a telephone exchange is required to achieve 50 to 100 years between breakdowns. We, therefore, developed techniques to lockout errors in either hardware or software by safeguarding computer memory in-depth and detail.

However, privacy and security coincide in defining the functional boundaries across which movement in or out must be controlled. Therefore, comprehensive privacy is also achieved by developing acceptable security based on named digital objects under lock and key because boundaries are aligned with digital functionality.

But I must return to construct my bridgehead. For this, I begin in ancient Egypt.

Slide 1 - Ancient Security Systems (The Pyramids)

Pharaohs required privacy in death and security in slumber. Their imposing architectural features and the impregnable physical superstructure provided an impressive solution. Subsequently, the pyramids were attacked and raided, but many internal chambers remained secret and safely hidden. The pyramids were state-of-the-art then, which is worth remembering in our search.

Slide 2 - Contrived Security (A Pole Sitter)

Contrived solutions exist, but their proprietary nature and eccentricity mean they are not constructed for everyday users. It is because they demand specialised skills, which are not universally appropriate, well understood or quickly grasped. Thus, contrived solutions are constantly hacked and unreliable, and the medieval castle typifies the acceptable solution.

Slide 3 - Functional Privacy and Security (Medieval City)

Functional privacy and security begin with solid, impregnable walls as natural fortifications. It started in Babylon at the birth of civilisation. A sheer, high wall adds to the physical strength. Guarded gates provide additional protection, creating domains of Baronial security, from village safety to family protection and even marital bliss, using further physical protection. Indeed, a chastity belt is the first example of a hardware solution to a software problem. (laughter)

Slide 4 - Universal Application of Physical Boundaries

Historically, all such solutions share the universal enclosed physical boundary strength principle. It is an all-enveloping hardware boundary turned for large or small objects. Total enclosures are private and secure areas for storing personal and private objects held safe by a lockbox, including complex executable objects such as a will, signed, stamped, and authorised by a trusted independent entity when created.

EMPLOYMENT OF WELL DEFINED PHYSICAL
HARDWARE BOUNDARIES

Slide 4.

Thus, the first observation concerning traditional standards is the explicit and physical nature of all boundaries, and the second is the variable size and scope of each private and secure object. Hand in hand is the need for limited, gated, dynamically controlled and typed access validation.

Slide 5 - Gated Access Rights (Guarded Castle Gate)

Returning to the medieval castle, the Baron provided only one or two castle gates, and every gate activity was guarded. At this point, we can recognise two complementary and reinforcing checks. Access requires advanced knowledge about the castle's location and a specific gate. Second, entry requests must pass the challenge of the guards who dynamically enforce pre-authorised lists crosscheck, confirm any expected passwords, and verify any key or token. Thus, the resulting traditional standard is locks and keys to enter a gate, a door, or a lid, guarded dynamically inside and outside as with any trusted, strong room.

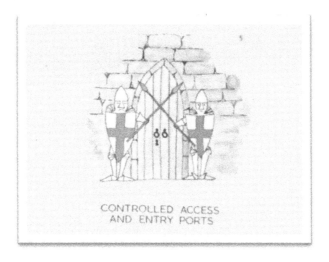

CONTROLLED ACCESS
AND ENTRY PORTS

Slide 5.

Slide 6 - Unavoidable Dynamic Checks

Of course, for privacy and security to be maintained, these checks must be performed continuously and dynamically, catching errors red-handedly on the spot. Error detection must occur in the event of any invalid request. After that, it is too late. Moreover, the rules must apply universally equally to all requests. No special privileges or any exceptions are tolerated. Even the Baron, another primitive, centralised operating system, must be subjected to the same controls. It is the only way to protect the software from corruption by or within the operating system.

DYNAMIC CHECKING MECHANISMS
UNIVERSALLY APPLIED

Slide 6.

Slide 7 - Independent Enforcement

As part of these dynamic standards, fault isolation and correction methods are needed to ensure the preservation and progress of law-and-order equality for all. Freedom and equality within the law are fundamental to democratic progress. It is only possible when law, order, speedy justice, and punishment apply transparently.

FAULT ISOLATION AND CORRECTION

Slide 7

Slide 8 – Golden Tokens of Ownership

Integrity is maintained through private ownership of individual tokens. The token bestows the authority to act as a private capability key. They are aided by a secret map, hidden locations, and additional keys or certificates of trusted authority that act like a badge of office or a mayor's chain democratically passed down over time to elected individuals. These tokens signify a right to act on specific objects or execute some democratically approved function.

A token authorises and translates an available capability into an approved action. The reality of approved access rights leads to a networked environment where action is only permitted on an object, given an approved need-to-know capability key with some limited modes. A capability is a key to accessing a secure object in some previously approved way. Thus, security and privacy are built on the tokens' integrity, keys, maps, passports, secret passwords, and hidden entry lists that approve access rights.

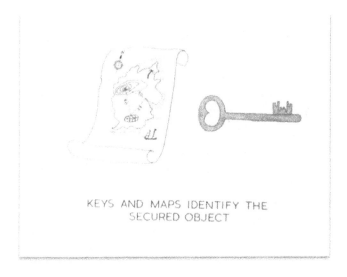

KEYS AND MAPS IDENTIFY THE
SECURED OBJECT

Slide 8

But the demands placed upon the tokens or capability keys are the same as demanded by the original object, no more and no less. Here, we come to an essential constraint in implementation. Privacy and security are only sustained if confidence is provided through the independence of the crosschecking mechanisms.

Slide 9 - A Common Currency

TOKENS OPERATE THROUGH INTEGRITY

Slide 9

Thus, the tokens are necessarily minted and maintained on a community basis as a hard currency. Tokens are abstract values with inherent and transparent integrity regarding the related object. It is always true, irrespective of the level of abstraction. For example, the difference between gold, cash, and checks is simply a different abstraction of wealth. A capability key provides the required hard currency built into computer hardware for addressing the wealth or value of objects stored in memory. The tokens are independently secured to prevent corruption through programmed forgery.

Slide 10 - Fail-safe Implementation

Slide 10.

Thus, a sixth observed need is for transparent and independent auditing by independent agencies. The success of each independent subsystem is most reinforcing when it begins at the instruction level of the computer. Each computer instruction is validated and verified by an independent meta-machine, a capability-based hardware checking mechanism.

Trust and confidence only increase with fail-safe mechanisms, a double-checking approach of reasonableness tests. This routine checking mechanism maintains trust by catching accidental and deliberate mistakes' red-handed.' This penultimate need maintains justice and equality under the law through independent, fail-safe policies in execution.

Slide 11 - Democratic Individual Freedoms

These restrictions do not mean a straitjacket. User freedom exists to determine the level of privacy and security on each object stored in computer memory and to define who can have what level of access to each private object. A distributed democratic, not a centralised, privileged dictatorial solution is achieved. Therefore, my final requirement concerning traditional or natural systems is uniform freedom of choice within democratic controls.

Slide 11.

Slide 12 – Putting Everything Together

These are my standards for socially acceptable computers claiming security and privacy. It introduces the complex details of secure hardware and confidential data. The Plessy PP250 implemented these requirements using capability-limited-addressing to the highest standards. Given the state-of-the-art, this can be summarised in four quadrants of a multi- dimensional graph of operations.

Moving clockwise and starting on the right, user-defined objects of variable size, scope, and complexity are locked up and only unlocked for some limited access by private capability keys. These immutable digital keys define some authority over the object held safe in locked, guarded memory locations.

Objects can only be accessed by owning a capability key to unlock the object. Complex objects are built from chains of individual, type-limited digital blocks. Executable programs, read or write data, and capability lists (key ring blocks) abstract programmed functions into secure, private domains. Domains are protected as subroutine methods that process files, devices, and other hidden implementation details at any level of software complexity.

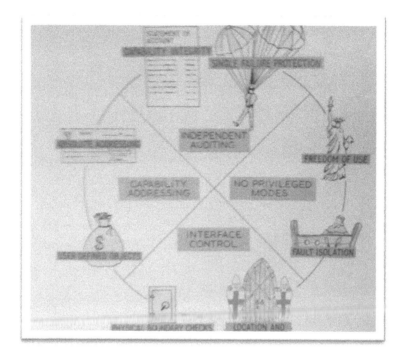

Slide 12.

Moving down, consider the physical strength in the lower quadrant. It is derived from hardware barriers checking the atomic actions of the system. Every machine instruction is checked, and each memory request is validated in advance (pipelined). A base and a limit address with specific, type-limited access modes define each block. The capability keys represent the independent, orthogonal scientific checks. Both location and access rights are verified.

The location is the object's current address range and geographic home in networked memory. Different users of the same object can have different access rights. One might need just read-only, while another might need write access. Critically, no default privileged modes exist. In the PP250, memory is never exposed to actions without in-line approval for a capability key. Most importantly, no centralised, highly privileged operating system breaks this rule.

Next, the left quadrant offers freedom to mint the hard, exchangeable currency as needed on demand. The keys have custom access rights to detect all errors. A single interpretation standard permits controlled exchange and movement without losing integrity, privacy, or security. Any attempted violation is detected on the spot and prevented dynamically by the validation hardware. Faulty elements are then isolated. Capability keys to both software domains and hardware equipment are trapped in use.

Because capability keys are immutable digital objects, they resist fraud and forgery. When keys are grouped into 'Enter-Only' capability lists as private domains, they form hierarchical chains as strings of fully protected functional hierarchical services. Security and privacy operate across complex, dynamic, programmed global communication networks. Key- based security ensures the need to know with the least privileged access right as the outside world expects.

Finally, most notably, to establish and sustain trust, it is necessary to implement logical integrity with independent auditing for fail-safe operations. PP250 engineered two independent programmable machines working in engineered harnesses to crosscheck each other's authority. The design guarantees that no single error can compromise memory integrity. A single failure, either in hardware or software, deliberate or accidental, is detected, and memory integrity is maintained.

These are the four quadrants on which to build and operate networks of secure computers running trusted software. It works because it considers privacy and security in line with functionality as individual atomic objects and how they interact. At every level, enforcing checks with physical hardware in a logical, programmed, independent manner guarantees functionality.

Let me go back and restate the need for engineers to apply these natural standards instead of the contrived general-purpose science computer. Society's conventions, judged by traditional standards, address the entire population. They do not depend upon specialists or complex skills only known to experts. Any system is only as secure as the weakest point, and confidence increases concerning the increased depth of functional crosschecks. It is the responsibility of all here today to drive the appropriate socially acceptable solution to this most critical matter.

Context: Session 14 - Privacy and Security Issues in Computer Communication[33]

Chairperson R. E. Lyons, Chief of the Computer Systems Division, Defence Communication Engineering Agency, Reston, Virginia, U.S.A.

Presentations:

1. The Potential Problem of Data Havens, and the Possible Need for an International Treaty on Information Management by Hon. Barry M. Goldwater Jr., House of Representatives, Washington, D.C., U.S.A.

2. Options in Transfrontier Data Protection by F. W. Honduras, The Council of Europe Strasbourg, Truchterheim, France

3. Data Quality by K. Aner, Member of the Swedish Parliament, Kungsangen, Sweden

4. Privacy Security and Control Problems in a Public Data Net Environment by T. Oswald, Head of Division, Data Inspection Board, Stockholm, Sweden

---

33   dblp: ICCC 1976 (dagstuhl.de)

5. A Comprehensive System for the Online Implementation of Privacy and Security Measures by K.J. Hamer-Hodges, Division Head, Plessey Telecommunications Ltd. Pool, Dorset, England

6th ACM Symposium on Operating System Principles – Session 3 Capability Panel

6th ACM Symposium on Operating System Principles
Session 3. Capability Panel
K. Hamer-Hodges   ITT
November 17, 1978

I must say at the outset that the ideas I express and the statements
I make are my own personal observations and should not be taken as
a statement of any corporate viewpoint.

To begin with, it is my experience that hardware based capability
addressing can be implemented as a commercial product not just
a research tool. The questions today are what should be selected?
How should it be implemented? and what can you expect to achieve?
I would like to concentrate upon the enter mechanism which I believe
is the most advantageous aspect of the capability system. Further,
to be dependable I believe this mechanism must be implemented in
hardware. To me an Enter capability identifies a real and actionable
object, it is at least a segment of memory space, not just a
protected value that only takes a significance when analyzed by some
special program.

An enter capability addresses a compartment as an instance of a
protected domain. Such a compartment will possess two certain
attributes. First it is insulated within the total system of
compartments due to the fact that each component segment is of known
size and location within the memory spectrum. Hardware checks maintain
this insulating mode by illuminating invalid references. As a result
a compartment's activities are contained and thus other compartments
are protected.

Figure 1. Second a domain has one or more procedural components.
The external operation that can be performed on an enter capability
switches the domains and transfers control in a secure way.

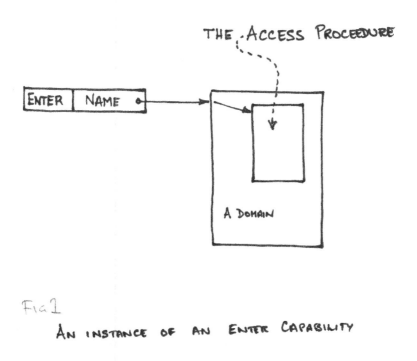

Figure 4 An Instance of an Enter Capability

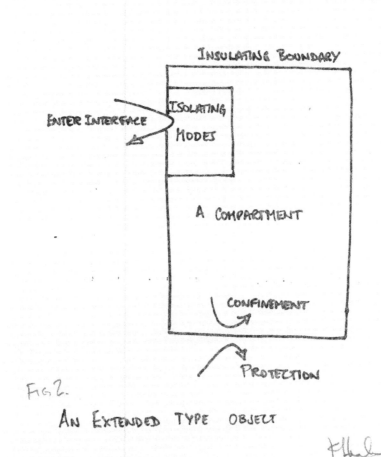

Figure 5 An Extended-Type Object

An access procedure isolates the domain from invalid
requests to access procedures of the new domain. By guarding the
domain interface and establishing the domain environment, it is not
possible to access any element of the domain without the transfer
of control taking place to validate the modes of operation.
Internally, the relationship is a set of procedures and data objects
and probably further enter capabilities. Each system must define
mechanisms which distinguish the distinct elements, however, such
formats should not be troublesome. Principally, the domain is self
controlled. A complier can make an excellent job of ensuring that
the self controlling modes of access among the components is as it
should be.

Figure 2. The enter capability mechanisms build upon the basic
protection afforded by the insulation and isolation attributes of
a domain to yield an extended type of object providing an element
or unit of abstraction within the design. Together the insulating and
isolating mechanisms give substance and confidence that the COMPARTMENTS
of the system are secured from abuse and from misuse.

The enter operation should be regarded as the only way to enter a
domain. In particular, it should not be possible to RETURN implicitly
to some assumed condition of a domain. Since to do so usurps the
isolating access program controls, the process of threading between
such domains must at all times be explicite. If control is surrendered
but is expected to be returned the envoking domain must pass explicitly
the enter capability to be used when control is to be returned. This
avoids the hazards of returning to an implied state when events
may occur to invalidate this assumption. Typically, this is the
situation between parallel asynchronous processes. However, I do not
believe that one need place the process onto a ready queue and
schedule in a conventional sense in every situation. To do so would
imply an unacceptable overhead in using the mechanisms. The action
of entering is all the scheduling that is required.

Using such a technique it is possible to construct small, even very small, independent domains each one fully in control of its state, its state changes and its environment. In particular, this mechanism will be seen to have direct significance in the construction of more complex processing architectures where a user process may thread itself throughout hardware and firmware, as well as software domains.

The full use of this implementation hiding properties of an enter capability can then be utilized not only to hide the particular software implementation but also the implementations that mechanize the domain.

Let me emphasize again these mechanisms must be implemented in hardware because only then can a reality be given to the insulation and the enter capability mechanisms. At the hardware level, the design can be assured to be failure independent and proveably so. Consequently, a system so designed is protected from any single fault leading to an undetected breakdown of the mechanisms.

Up to now, technical difficulties and conflicting commercial advantages have delayed progress. This delay is self perpetuating because it leaves unchecked the inertia of common practice. Applied appropriately, the power and elegance of the capability mechanisms can remove many of our current system problems. There are no special cases in a design built upon a hardware enter capability mechanisms. All elements of a design conform to this same atomic structure. In such a way the enter capability becomes the looking glass to our own wonderlands. And if I may make a prediction the enter operation can become a candidate for a Class Ø operating system.

ABOUT THE AUTHOR

Author Kenneth J. Hamer-Hodges stands at the forefront of computer science as an esteemed author and renowned computer security expert distinguished by his pioneering work in fail-safe computer science. Hamer-Hodges has dedicated his decades of expertise to addressing the critical challenges posed by the advent of superhuman artificial intelligence and its implications for digital society. His insightful and groundbreaking publications on civilizing cyberspace reflect his deep understanding of technology's evolving role in shaping democratic societies. Hamer-Hodges' unique blend of technical prowess and visionary thinking makes him a leading voice in the discourse on cybersecurity and the future of AI at the crossroads between technology and society.

He remains an independent consultant in South Florida, working on secure cloud-based and mobile access software. He graduated in the UK, where he developed the microprograms for the first Capability-Based Computers (PP250), became a Chartered Engineer, was awarded a Fellowship of the IEE (London), and partnered on a dozen patents developing Object Engineering fundamentals while working in the UK, USA, Germany, and Belgium, and as an invitation speaker at conferences on Operating Systems, Communication systems, and digital security.

OTHER BOOKS BY THE AUTHOR

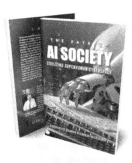

The Fate of AI Society: Civilizing Superhuman Cyberspace

"The Fate of AI Society by Kenneth Hamer-Hodges is a compelling exploration of the convergence of surveillance, digital technology, and democracy, drawing inspiration from George Orwell's seminal work 1984. The book adeptly warns against the perils of centralized power and advocates for decentralization using λ-calculus, Capability-Based addressing, and object-oriented programming to empower individuals and mitigate cyber threats." Review of The Fate of AI Society Post by Ramadevi Tatavarthi » 26 Feb 2024, 09:23

Civilizing Cyberspace: The Fight For Digital Democracy

"Civilizing Cyberspace: The Fight for Digital Democracy is a non-fiction book by Kenneth Hamer-Hodges using the first person. It explains to readers why we are at a turning point when it comes to cybersecurity because the point of singularity, when computer software outsmarts humanity, is near. In this context, if the fundamental architecture of computers doesn't change, "we head for national cyber-catastrophe." Using several concrete examples, Hamer-Hodges shows us how malware and other digital threats undermine democracy itself."
Official Review: Civilizing Cyberspace
Post OnLineBookClub.com, 26 Jun 2020, 14:19

www.ingramcontent.com/pod-product-compliance
Lightning Source LLC
La Vergne TN
LVHW011803070326
832902LV00031B/4650